Christmas Hostage

JANE BLYTHE

Acknowledgments

I'd like to thank everyone who played a part in bringing this story to life. Particularly my mom who is always there to share her thoughts and opinions with me. My wonderful cover designer Amy who did an amazing job with this stunning cover. My fabulous editor Mitzi for all the hard work she puts into polishing my work. My awesome team, Sophie, Robyn, and Clayr, without your help I'd never be able to run my street team. And my fantastic street team members who help share my books with every share, comment, and like!

And of course a big thank you to all of you, my readers! Without you I wouldn't be living my dreams of sharing the stories in my head with the world!

CHAPTER *One*

December 18th
7:11 P.M.

These long days were going to kill her.

Well, not really, but Hannah was so tired. Running a business on her own was a lot more work than she'd ever thought it would be. And she had thought it would be a lot of work. Still, she wouldn't change a single thing. She was living her dream. Work wise at least.

Her personal life was pretty much a mess.

"That's everything in the safe, Hannah."

"Already? You guys are so quick. Thanks, Jeff; you're a lifesaver." Hannah smiled up at the older man. She was so grateful she had him; he worked hard and he'd filled in the occasional time she got sick and couldn't make it in. If she didn't have Jeff Shields, she didn't think she could make her business the success it was.

"You should go home early tonight," he told her.

"Maybe," she nodded noncommittally.

Jeff laughed. "You're not going to, are you?"

"I have so much work to do." Running a jewelry store was busy enough as it was, but it was a week out from Christmas, and things had been crazy. She'd been working from six in the morning until nine or ten at night, every night, then driving home in a fog to eat and collapse into bed before getting up and doing it all over again. Still, there was only one more week to go until Christmas. Then, after all the holiday hoopla calmed down, things would quiet down a little before picking up again in the lead up to Valentine's Day.

"You're going to burn yourself out." Jeff's brown eyes were full of concern.

So, what? she thought to herself. There was no one to worry about her if she did. And besides, when she kept herself busy, she kept herself out of the dark place that used to consume her. She wasn't going back there. Ever. So, she focused all her energy on her work, and it was paying off. Her store was booming.

"Do you want me to go pick up something for you to eat for dinner and drop it off before I go home?" Jeff offered.

"That's so sweet, but . . ." Hannah trailed off as movement on the CCTV screen caught her eye.

Then she froze.

Jeff's gaze followed hers, and he gasped.

Two armed men in balaclavas had just walked through the front door of the store.

Hannah's every instinct clambered at her to run and hide, to flee to safety. But she and Jeff weren't the only ones here. Her other employee, nineteen-year-old Vincent Zimmerman, was still in the workroom. Her office was at the back of the store, but the workroom was between it and the main storeroom. If she didn't warn Vincent and get him back here where they could escape out the back door, then the armed robbers would get him.

"Hannah, no." Jeff grabbed for her arm as she ran past him.

She shook him off. She couldn't stay here and let Vincent get hurt. How would she live with herself if he was killed?

Triggering the silent alarm that would bring the police running and ignoring the back door that led to safety, Hannah threw open the office door and froze again.

She was too late.

The two men stood in her workroom.

Her vision tunneled until all it saw were the guns in their hands.

She had a massive phobia of guns.

They terrified her.

Paralyzed her.

She would have bolted from the room regardless of the consequences if only she had control of her body.

"What's the code to the safe?"

Hannah heard the words, but she couldn't seem to make sense of them. In her head, they got all muddled up, then finally put themselves back together.

The code.

They wanted the code.

If she gave it to them, then they'd just take what they wanted and leave.

She tried to say the numbers, but her mouth refused to form the words.

"The code," one of the men growled, pointing his gun at Vincent.

"I don't know, man, I don't know," Vincent whimpered. "Only she does." He gestured at her.

"What's the code, lady?"

She wanted to answer.

She really did.

Her mouth moved but no sound came out.

Her stock wasn't worth someone's life. Diamonds, gold, rubies, emeralds, sapphires—it wasn't anything her insurance wouldn't cover.

Panic was swimming inside her, filling her up, growing exponentially by the second. They were going to shoot Vincent if she didn't say something.

"What is the code?"

The taller of the two men stalked toward her, and she began to shake in fear. Now was not the time to let her phobia of guns turn her into a mute. She had to tell them. Then they could take what they wanted and leave before anyone got hurt.

"Do you *want* me to blow your brains out?" The man yanked her up against a chest as solid as steel and rammed the gun into her temple.

She knew what the cold, smooth metal of a gun barrel felt like against her bare flesh.

She had felt it before, barely making it through that night alive, and now, she feared this time she wouldn't be so lucky.

"Just shoot her," the other man said.

"Then how are we gonna get the code?" the one pressing a gun to her head snapped.

"Shoot her in the foot, and see if that makes her talk."

Hannah whimpered and her shaking intensified.

"You hear that, lady?" The man shoved the gun into her temple so hard she knew it would leave a bruise, which would be the least of her problems if they started firing it. "You don't tell us the code in the next five seconds, I'm gonna shoot you in the leg. Then I'm gonna shoot you in the other leg. Then I'm gonna move on to your arms. Get the idea?" he snarled.

"One, two," the other man started counting as though this were all just some big joke to them.

Tell them, Hannah commanded herself.

"Three, four."

Now, they were about to start shooting.

"I'll tell you the code."

Jeff appeared in the doorway of the office. She'd thought he had escaped out the back door and gotten to safety. Why hadn't he gone? Now they were going to kill him, too. Jeff didn't know the code to the safe where they stored the most expensive jewelry overnight. She was the only one who did. That had always seemed like the safest option. Now that decision might cost all of them their lives.

"What's the code, old man?" the robber holding her asked, digging the gun harder against her temple.

"It's seven, two, nine, five," Jeff replied.

"Open it." The man finally moved the gun from her head, and Hannah sighed in relief.

That relief was short lived.

When they tried to open the safe and found the code Jeff had given them didn't work, they were going to start shooting.

Why had Jeff come in here?

He should have run when he had the chance.

Now he was going to die, too.

All because she couldn't speak.

"It didn't work." The man at the safe turned back to his partner.

"You think you can lie to us, old man?" The gun was shoved against her ribcage, and Hannah prepared herself to die.

The bang was amplified in her head.

She waited for the accompanying shaft of agony.

Only it didn't come.

Then she realized why.

Jeff was on the floor, a bright red patch of blood blooming on his chest.

They hadn't shot her; instead, they'd shot her friend.

He was dying.

She had to do something or Vincent would be next.

Then she heard the most magical sound in the world.

Sirens.

Growing louder.

Getting closer.

Help was coming.

It would arrive any second.

Seemingly realizing this, the two men cursed, and then she was released and they were fleeing through the office.

With the gun out of sight, Hannah regained control of her body and flung herself down next to Jeff. Was he still alive? She pressed her fingertips to his neck and felt his pulse thumping steadily beneath them.

"Get me something to stop the bleeding," she screamed to Vincent who still stood in the same place he'd been in when the armed robbers burst in. "Vince, something to stop the bleeding," she repeated, then added more gently, "they're gone."

The teenager blinked slowly, his dark eyes two big saucers in his pale face. Then he nodded slowly and left the room.

Hannah whipped her attention back to Jeff; he was paler than

Vincent, and his breath was wheezing in and out. *He couldn't die.* She would never forgive herself if he died because of her. Why hadn't she just answered the robbers and given them the code? Her phobia could have gotten her killed. Her and two other innocent people.

"Here." Vincent dropped a coat at her side.

She snatched it up and pressed it hard against Jeff's wound. She was rewarded with a groan of pain and prayed that meant he was going to live. It had to be a good thing, right? He was conscious enough to feel pain. And help was almost here. They would rush Jeff to the hospital and fix him. Save him. He wasn't going to die. He wasn't. He couldn't.

"Move out of the way, ma'am."

Large hands gently clasped hers and pulled them away from Jeff's chest, then moved to her shoulders and pulled her to her feet.

She hadn't heard the cops arrive.

She was pushed carefully to the side as the two officers began to perform first aid.

As she stared at Jeff's still face, everything else faded around her.

All she thought about was willing him to keep breathing.

Her face was wet with tears. She could feel them falling like drops of ice down her cold cheeks. Her hands were wet and sticky with Jeff's blood. Her entire body trembled.

The wait for the EMTs felt like an eternity.

Eventually, they arrived. They tended to Jeff's wound, started an IV, checked his vitals, and bundled him onto a stretcher and out of the store.

She stared after them.

Maybe people were talking to her. Maybe they were asking her if she was all right. Maybe they were asking her what had happened. She wasn't really sure.

Her legs could no longer support her, and Hannah's knees buckled and she sank to the floor.

~

8:32 P.M.

. . .

"Are you sure the owner of the shop's name is Hannah Buffy?" Special Agent Tom Drake asked his partner.

Chloe rolled her eyes at him. "Yes. Just like I was sure the last five million times you asked. Why? Who is Hannah Buffy?"

Tom just shook his head.

Hannah was long gone, no longer part of his life, and this woman had to be someone else who just happened to share her name.

"This is the fifth burglary in the last month," Chloe said, assuming he wasn't going to elaborate on who Hannah was.

"They're getting bolder," he said, pushing all thoughts of Hannah from his mind. "This is the first time they hurt someone."

"It is. And they didn't even get hardly anything," Chloe said. "First cops on the scene said they fled with only a handful of jewelry."

"Could mean they're going to hit another store sooner rather than later," he said as he parked the car among the many others outside a small jewelry store. If it weren't for the half a dozen cop cars, crime scene truck, and ambulance, the strip mall would have been beautiful. It was full of high-end stores where a pair of jeans cost more than he made in a month, and with what you'd pay for even the cheapest meal at any of the restaurants, he could have fed himself and his entire extended family for the week. The stores were quaint, and the street was lined with trees, which had been strung with hundreds of fairy lights. Snowflakes were fluttering in the air, covering everything with a light dusting of snow.

Hannah had loved Christmastime. He wondered if she still did or if, like with him, nothing had been the same since things between them ended.

Deliberately, Tom ordered himself to stop thinking about Hannah. He hadn't in months, it was just hearing her name that had brought back the memories.

No, that was a lie.

He thought about her every day.

Every. Single. Day.

But this wasn't about Hannah.

He was here to do his job.

Nothing more, nothing less.

Then he walked inside.

And came face-to-face with the woman whose grip on his heart he had never been able to loosen.

He had known that it couldn't be anyone else. He'd been clinging to the delusion that this had nothing to do with her, but how many women named Hannah Buffy could there be who owned a jewelry store? Of course, it was her.

Hannah was sitting on the floor, in a corner of the room, her eyes closed, her head resting back against the wall, her knees drawn up to her chest. Her face was pale, and her long dark auburn hair hung around her shoulders. She was wearing a black dress that clung to her frame—which was thinner than the last time he'd see her—and black, knee-high boots.

Even from across the room, he could see the blood on her hands and the tear tracks on her cheeks.

Blood.

His eyes zeroed in and locked onto it.

The sight of blood didn't bother him.

Unless it was on Hannah.

That he couldn't stand.

That made him sick to his stomach.

That made him want to tear his hair out and find who was responsible for putting the blood on her and then rip them to shreds.

"Why didn't someone clean her up?" he demanded.

"She won't let anyone go near her," the closest cop replied.

Tonight would have been traumatic enough being held at gunpoint, but given Hannah's history, it would have been infinitely more horrifying. Just knowing what she had been put through had his heart thumping painfully in his chest. "Has an EMT checked her out?"

"No. They tried, she refused. She hasn't done anything but sit there and cry."

"You know her," Chloe said quietly.

Tom nodded. He knew Hannah *very* well, indeed. And he wasn't letting her sit there and relive the trauma that had torn them apart any longer.

He walked over and stood above her. She didn't notice him. Just sat there. Alone. Trapped in memories. He didn't have to ask her to know what she would be thinking about.

"Hannah," he said softly.

Her eyes popped open, and she looked up at him, her mouth falling open in shock. Tom loved those eyes. Depending on her mood they could be as bright a blue as the sky on a hot summer's day, green like the ocean, or a bleak, desolate gray. Right now, they were gray, representing the atmosphere around them. She stared at him for a long moment then squeezed her eyes closed and opened them again, apparently, wondering if he were nothing more than an apparition. As though she may have conjured him up right out of her mind. He knew seeing him again was as big a shock for her as it was for him to see her.

Up close, Tom could see a bruise forming on her temple. A round circle of black and blue. It was the barrel of the gun. It may have been three years since they'd divorced, but Tom felt the familiar rush of protective rage flash through him at the thought of anyone hurting Hannah.

Quickly, his gaze skimmed her body in search of any other injuries. She hadn't been checked out by a paramedic so there could be injuries they didn't know about yet. He didn't see anything else other than the blood on her dress as well as her hands, but he assumed the blood was her employee's. When the first cops arrived on the scene they had found Hannah on her knees beside the older gentleman, keeping pressure on his gunshot wound.

Although she appeared to be mostly uninjured, what he was most concerned about was her going into shock. Tremors wracked her body in a constant steady stream. Tom shrugged out of his coat, but when he bent down to drape it over her shoulders, she shrunk away from him.

"You're shaking, Hannah," he reprimanded. "I'm scared you're going into shock."

Her big eyes just stared at him, but she didn't shrink away from him again as he wrapped his coat around her. With the heavy material draped over her, Hannah's shaking calmed a little and her hands grasped the lapels of the coat and pulled it tighter.

Her bloodstained hands.

Before he could interview her, he needed to get that blood off her hands. He hated seeing blood on her; it brought back too many memories of a day he'd much rather forget. Leaving Hannah where she was, he went and found the bathroom where he wet a towel and then returned to her.

Crouching at her side, he grasped one of Hannah's hands and began to clean it. Part of him expected her to pull away, refuse to let him touch her like she had the last time they had been in the same room together. But she didn't. She just sat there and trembled and watched as he washed as much of the blood from her hands as he could.

There was blood on her face, too. She had big smears on her cheeks where she must have brushed her bloody hands against them at some point. Taking hold of her chin, he angled her face so he could wipe away the blood that was there.

Hannah's big eyes grew bigger as he leaned in closer to make sure he had gotten all the blood off. Her breath was warm against his face, and he drew in the scent of her. A mixture of the cherry scented shampoo she always used and the vanilla perfume that was her favorite. The combination of the two reminded him of the cherry pies his grandmother used to make every Sunday when he was a child.

It felt so good to be touching her after so long.

But she wasn't his to touch anymore.

He should release her.

Instead, of their own accord, his fingers reached up and brushed across her damp cheeks, catching the tears that were still falling. His fingertips lingered there, not wanting to break physical contact with her, for his sake as much as hers.

But at last, Tom let his hand fall away, and since he had her mostly cleaned up, he sat back on his haunches and studied her. She was ashen, her pupils dilated, her skin clammy, and when he had brushed his fingertips over her wrist while he'd been washing her hands he had felt her pulse beating way too fast.

She was in shock.

She needed to be examined and treated.

"Are you okay?" he asked. He knew it was a stupid question. How could she be okay? But he needed to hear her talk. He needed to reassure himself that she was, in fact, all right. That she was strong enough to endure this just as she had endured everything else that had been thrown at her.

Hannah nodded.

Tom shook his head back at her. "Of course, you're not okay." He kept his voice quiet so only she could hear him. "They held a *gun* on you, Hannah." Again, moving of its own volition, his hand moved to trace the darkening bruise on her temple.

This time she did flinch away from his touch, and he quickly snatched his hand back.

She looked so small and scared and fragile, and he had to remind himself that Hannah was none of those things. She was the toughest person he knew. What she had been through would crush most people, and yet she had survived. And by the looks of her store, survived and thrived. Well, thrived businesswise. She was too thin and there were dark smudges under her eyes that he knew had nothing to do with the night's events.

Sometimes Hannah was *too* strong. She thought she could handle everything on her own, and acted like admitting you needed help was a bad thing.

"I want to call the EMTs over to check you out," he told her.

"I'm not hurt," Hannah said. Hearing her voice again made him shiver. Even scared and traumatized, her voice was the sweetest and most melodic sound he'd ever heard.

"You're in shock; you should be examined," he countered.

"No."

Tom sighed. That was his stubborn girl.

Then he sighed again. She wasn't his girl anymore. She wasn't his concern. Her emotional well-being was none of his business, just the way she wanted it. He was here to do a job, that was all. And to that end, he needed to interview her to find out what exactly had happened here tonight. He would be able to get more out of her once she wasn't so preoccupied with the blood on the carpet and replaying in her mind everything that had gone on in this room tonight.

"Do you think you can stand up?"

Hannah shook her head.

"I want to get you out of this room, okay?" He spoke slowly, making sure her shock-muddled brain was hearing him. "You shouldn't be in here looking at your friend's blood. I'll help you up." Tom stood and extended his hand.

She didn't move. In her face, he could clearly see she was debating her options. She knew he was taking her out of the room regardless of any protest she offered, and she knew her legs most likely weren't steady enough to support her, but she didn't want to accept his help. For some reason, the notion of letting him help her was repulsive to her.

Eventually, she sighed, and having weighed her options, she grasped his hand and let him pull her to her feet. As soon as she was standing, she tugged her hand free, and just as he had suspected, her legs weren't strong enough to hold her upright now. She teetered, then staggered forward and lost her balance, landing in his outstretched arms.

~

9:04 P.M.

Hannah knew as soon as she was on her feet that standing up had been a bad idea. She wobbled all over the place. Seeking something solid.

Then her knees buckled and she fell.

Landing in a strong pair of arms.

Arms that wrapped around her in a comforting warmth of familiarity and safety.

She was pulled against a rock-hard chest, and although she knew it was a bad idea, she rested against it, letting those arms hold her up. Her head swam, and her stomach turned in a constant procession of slow somersaults. She wanted to move away, to stand on her own two feet, but she knew that right now that was out of the question.

Tom Drake.

What were the chances that her ex-husband would turn up here tonight?

The odds had to be astronomical.

And yet, here he was.

Holding her, soothing her fears, calming her pounding heart, guiding her shock-addled brain back to reality.

This was wrong.

She had to get away from him. Letting him hold her was only going to make this so much harder than it was already going to be.

Lifting her hands to Tom's chest, she pushed until he loosened his hold. When he didn't release her, she tipped her head back so she could look up at him. The light brown eyes that stared back at her were swirling with emotion, but then he shuttered them and they went blank.

Hannah felt her heart drop.

Nothing had changed.

She was stupid for allowing herself to believe for even a second that things could be different.

When she pushed at his chest again, Tom let his arms drop to his sides this time. She took a step backward, and was swamped by a rush of dizziness so severe she could do nothing but moan and crumple.

Again, when she fell, her landing was in the same pair of strong arms.

This time they swung her feet up off the ground and carried her out of her store.

As soon as they stepped out into the night and the cold air hit her, Hannah felt the cobwebs begin to clear from her head. The blood was gone, the gun was gone, the fear that had held her in its icy grasp began to lessen, and she felt herself returning to her usual self.

"Put me down, Tom," she ordered, pleased when her voice sounded strong and confident, not the weak, quivering mess it had been before.

"You fainted, Hannah," he shot back, his voice harsh.

"I'm okay," she said firmly.

"Fine. Whatever." He let her slide slowly down his body till her feet touched the ground, then kept his arm around her waist until he was sure she had her bearings.

When Tom finally withdrew his arm, she very nearly toppled over again, but through sheer strength of will managed to remain on her feet and fairly steady. She drew in long, slow, deep breaths of the winter air and slowly, bit by bit the dizziness began to fade.

She was still shaking, though; she hadn't been able to quell it since she first saw the guns.

Guns.

For a moment, it all came rushing back. The fear, the panic, how close she had come to dying.

If the cops hadn't shown up when they did, she would be dead right now.

Jeff could still die.

And all because she had frozen.

"Your friend will be okay." Although it had been three years since they'd divorced, apparently Tom was still able to read in her face what she was thinking. "The bullet missed his heart and his lungs," he continued, turning her to face him, taking hold of one of her arms and slipping it into the sleeves of his coat, which was still draped around her shoulders. As he slipped her other arm in and buttoned it up, dressing her as though she were a child, he said, "He was lucky. A couple of inches either way, and he could have died instantly."

She shivered.

So close.

So close to dying.

Hannah had to push the thoughts away before they consumed her. The cops *had* come, and their sirens *had* scared the robbers off, and all of them *had* made it out alive.

"I'm going to take you over to get checked out by the medics," Tom announced.

That snapped her back to her senses. She wasn't hurt. She didn't need a doctor. "I told you I was okay."

"You have a bruise." He lifted his hand as though to touch the mark like he had done back in her store, but this time his hand stopped before it made contact with her skin.

"It's nothing. He just shoved the gun into my head. I'll be fine," she insisted.

"Hannah, you were held hostage, with a gun to your head. A *gun*. You know you need to be checked out." He sounded annoyed. She was *very* good at annoying Tom.

She couldn't think about the gun right now. If Tom was here, then the FBI was involved. She'd heard about the other armed robberies at jewelry stores throughout the city. Whatever else Tom was or was not, he was a good agent, and he would find these men before anyone else got hurt, but to do that, he would need her statement. She wanted to just do it and get it over with, then go home, swallow some sleeping pills, and go to sleep.

"I'll give you my statement first."

"Hannah," he frowned at her.

"I'm not arguing with you, Tom. Ask me whatever questions you have, and then I'll let a medic look me over before I go home."

"Well, we're not doing it out here. We'll sit in the back of my car." He took her arm with a gentleness that was at odds with the irritated tone.

He had been so gentle with her inside, too. The way he had cradled each of her hands as he wiped the blood off them had caused a fresh wave of tears to cascade down her cheeks. No one had ever been as gentle with her as Tom had. Then when he had turned his attention to cleaning her face, she had wanted nothing more than to curl up in those arms that had at one time been her only solace when the world was crumbling around her.

"Here you go." He had steered her to a dark sedan, and now opened the door and guided her into the back seat. He closed the door then walked around to the other side and climbed in. A woman with shoulder-length light brown hair climbed into the driver's seat, turned on the engine, and then the heater. "You're still shaking, Hannah," Tom said, his voice soft again.

She didn't need to tell him that being held at gunpoint was the cause. He knew it. He knew why she had a phobia about guns. He knew everything about her.

"Chloe, can you get me some blankets?" he addressed the young woman in the front seat, his eyes never leaving hers. Once they were alone, he searched her face. "Are you really okay? I know how horrible that must have been for you."

New tears were clogging her throat. She didn't want to think about the night that she knew was seared into both of their minds forever. She wanted to erase it from her memory and her life, just like she wanted to forget tonight. "They shot Jeff because of me. Because I couldn't give them the code," she whispered.

Tom's eyes went fierce. "That is not your fault, Hannah. You know that. You still freeze up at the sight of a gun?"

When his gaze dropped down to his waist, hers followed. She saw the bulge under his sweater and knew it was his weapon. Involuntarily, her shaking intensified. She knew Tom would never use his gun on her, but now that he had drawn her attention to it, she couldn't look away.

"Do you want me to give it to Chloe and ask her to stay outside while we talk?"

She shook her head, her eyes still fixed firmly on Tom's waist.

"Hannah." He hooked a finger under her chin and forcibly— although carefully so as not to hurt her—tilted her face up. "I'm so sorry you had to go through that. I'm sorry I didn't find them before they hit your store."

That was the Tom she knew.

The man who took responsibility for everything that happened around him.

The man who wanted to save everyone even when they didn't need saving.

"I'll be okay," she reminded him. And she would. She was scared and she was in shock, but she would get through it. She was strong.

"I know you will." He gave her a half smile.

His eyes were just unshuttering when his partner returned, passing a stack of blankets to Tom. Hannah expected him to wrap them around her, but instead he simply passed them to her, his eyes empty again. She took them and wrapped both around herself, cocooning herself in a little bundle of warmth. Warmth that couldn't seem to penetrate through to the cold deep inside her.

"What time did you close up tonight?" Tom asked.

"Seven."

"Did you lock the front door?"

"No."

"Do you have any other employees?"

"Just Jeff and Vincent who were there with me."

"What did you do when you closed up?"

"I went to the office to start on paperwork." Tom's questions were helping her to calm down. Focusing on facts meant she didn't focus on her emotions. He had always been a details man. It made him good at his job but also hard to live with sometimes. He wanted to plan everything out, down to the tiniest detail, and when he lost that sense of control, he didn't know what to do.

"What did the others do?"

"They put all of our most expensive jewelry into the safe like we do every night."

"Do they have the code to the safe?"

"No, but they don't need it. I open it and then they put everything away and close it when they're done."

"You triggered the silent alarm at seven nineteen. Is it usual to have everything packed away in the safe that quickly?"

"It was maybe a little quicker than usual."

"How did you know the robbers were there?"

"I saw them on the CCTV screen in my office."

"Why didn't you leave? You could have run out the back door. Why did you stay?"

The first hint of emotion edged into Tom's voice. Whatever had happened between them, he still cared about her. Just not enough to have stayed. He had turned his back on her, walked away when she needed him the most. She couldn't forget that. "Vincent was still in there."

"You were in the workroom when the cops arrived. Did you go in there or did the robbers take you in there?"

"I went in. I thought I could warn Vincent before they got there."

"What did you see when you walked in?"

Hannah shivered as the scene recreated itself in her mind. "Two men with guns."

"Are you sure it was two men?"

"Yes."

"What did they say?" Tom's voice had gone soft again.

"They wanted the code. I wanted to give it to them. No amount of jewelry is worth someone's life. But I couldn't make my mouth work."

"How much is the stuff in the safe worth?"

"A couple of million, maybe."

"A couple of million?" Tom repeated, his eyes growing wide.

She just shrugged. She didn't care about that right now, not while Jeff was in a hospital because of her.

"Did the men address each other with names?"

"I don't think so."

"What about you or either of your employees, did they use your names?"

She thought, but wasn't sure, the gun had blocked out everything else from her mind. "I don't think so."

"What was their demeanor like? Were they calm? Were they anxious or nervous? Were there any arguments between them?"

She dropped her eyes to her lap, feeling useless that she couldn't answer any of those questions. "I don't know. All I saw were the guns."

"Did Jeff come into the room with you?"

"No. I thought he'd gotten away. I was surprised when he came in."

"Why did he come in?"

"He gave them a code."

"I thought only you had the code."

Hannah nodded. "He made one up. They got angry; that's why they shot him." Her breath hitched as the sound of the gunshot rang in her head.

"Why did they leave?"

"The sirens. We heard the sirens, and they just left. I ran to Jeff as soon as they were gone. There was so much blood. I thought he was going to die, because he had tried to save me. They were going to start shooting me until I gave them the code. There was so much blood," she intoned, remembering the feel of it on her hands as it seeped through the coat she'd held to Jeff's wound.

"But he's going to be okay," Tom reminded her. "Did you get a look at them?"

She shook her head. "They wore jeans and black hoodies. They had balaclavas on so I couldn't see their faces. I'm sorry, Tom, I don't have anything helpful to give you."

"You did fine." He patted her shoulder reassuringly. "Okay, interview is over for now. You can give an official statement in the morning. Now, you go and get checked out, then you go home and get some rest. Is there someone who can stay with you tonight?"

"I'll be fine on my own." All she wanted was to sleep. Adrenalin was draining from her system leaving her exhausted.

"Of course, you will." Terseness was back in Tom's tone. For some reason, he didn't like her to be self-sufficient. It had been a regular argument between them those last few weeks of their marriage. "I'll walk you to the ambulance. Don't even think about arguing," he snapped when she opened her mouth to protest.

There was no point in arguing. It wasn't worth it. She was too tired. Hannah climbed out of the car and was unsurprised that Tom was already there, ready to take her arm and help keep her on her feet.

At the back of the ambulance she went to unwrap the blankets that were still around her shoulders, but Tom stopped her. "Keep them, you're still shaking."

"What about your jacket?"

"Keep it. You can give it back to me tomorrow when you come to give your statement."

The thought of seeing Tom again tomorrow wasn't an altogether pleasant one. He stirred up too many unresolved feelings and emotions. Things had ended abruptly, and she could admit to herself that she still had unresolved issues with their breakup.

As medics bundled her up into the ambulance, Hannah watched Tom walk away.

He was here only because this was his job.

When it was over, he would walk away again.

She hoped her heart could handle it.

~

11:57 P.M.

Eat or go straight to bed.

Neither option sounded particularly appealing.

Tom locked the door behind him and tossed his keys on the table in the hall, and then stood and stared at his dark, empty house. He'd moved in here shortly after he and Hannah split up, neither of them had been able to stay in their house after what had happened there.

Although it had been three years since he'd bought the town-house, it had never felt like a home. He hadn't furnished it with more than the basics. The big open plan living, dining, and kitchen had nothing more than a single sofa and a TV—that he never watched—on an entertainment stand. There was no dining table. When he ate here, he sat on the one stool at the breakfast bar. Although the house had three bedrooms, two sat empty, and the master contained only his bed.

This was his house, not his home.

He hated living alone. He hated coming back from work after a long day and being met with nothing but silence. When he and Hannah had lived together, he'd come home each night to all the lights blazing, the smell of a home-cooked meal wafting out to meet him, and if he was lucky, Hannah would have baked something special.

It wasn't that he wanted a woman at home to take care of him. He had helped Hannah build her business and encouraged her in any way he could, and he had loved that she was smart and successful. Coming home to *her* was what had mattered. She had made their house a home, she had made his day better—no matter how bad it had been—just by being there.

Now without her, Tom felt so empty.

Letting her go had been the hardest thing he had ever done, but at the time it had felt like the only option. They had become poison to each other, taking a bad situation and making it so much worse. They had bickered constantly. Long, bitter arguments that left Hannah in tears and him feeling like the most useless human being on the planet.

It had been hard to accept that he wasn't helping his wife; he was hurting her.

It had been harder to accept that Hannah didn't need him.

What she needed was to be free of him.

She wanted to do it on her own. That had been her choice, and one that he had had to accept for both their sakes.

So, he had walked away.

It had nearly killed him, but he had done it because he had loved

Hannah enough to do what was best for her, even if that meant being away from him.

Did he still love Hannah?

Yes.

He didn't even have to consider that. He would *always* love her. She was the one great love of his life. He hadn't really dated since they had split up, only the occasional relationship that never went anywhere because his heart just wasn't in it. They had been nice women—pretty, funny, sweet, smart, sexy.

They could have made him happy if he had let them, but his heart was still tangled up in Hannah Buffy.

Seeing her tonight looking so small and scared and fragile brought back so many bad memories. Holding her in his arms when she had fainted had brought back a mixture of good and bad memories. Tom had loved carrying her curled against his chest, and when they used to go for hikes, Hannah had hated crossing streams, so he'd always picked her up and carried her across them. But the last few times he'd held her in his arms, it had been to comfort her as she relived the horror of what had happened to her.

A horror that would be brought back by tonight's events.

Maybe he shouldn't have left her alone.

The whole time he was interviewing her, he had been debating whether he should stay with her while she was examined by the paramedics, then personally see her safely home. She was holding it together surprisingly well, but he knew inside she must be a mess.

Inside *he* was a mess.

The thought of anyone hurting Hannah made his blood boil.

The thought of anyone holding a gun against her beautiful, soft skin rendered him useless.

But now wasn't the time to be rendered useless.

Now was the time to be focused and on his game. The robbery at Hannah's store was different than the other four. And if it was different, then there was a chance that it wasn't related. And if it wasn't related, then it meant that the jewelry might not have been the main goal. And if the jewelry wasn't the main goal, then something else was. And Tom was terrified that the something else could be Hannah herself.

He couldn't stomach the thought of her in any sort of danger.

He wouldn't allow it.

And if he let the past suck him back into that same cycle that had almost destroyed both Hannah and himself, then she could wind up paying the price, and that was unacceptable.

All he had to do was keep the focus on work.

He was here to do a job. And do his job, he would. He would find who had held Hannah and her co-workers at gunpoint and he would arrest them. Then she would be safe.

Although things were over between them, and they could never go back to the way they'd been before, he wished her all the best. He wanted her to be happy. He wanted her to find someone who could be the partner she needed. He wanted her to get married and have children and live out the rest of her life happy and at peace.

Maybe seeing her again, as hard as it was, was for the best.

Things had ended so abruptly that neither of them had really gotten any closure. Back when they got divorced, they had both been so raw, in so much pain, still traumatized by what had happened. Then they had decided to end their marriage and that was it. They hadn't seen each other again until tonight.

But now they could get that closure.

Now they could tie up any lingering feelings that still existed. They could say their goodbyes properly, so this time when they walked away, they would both be able to move on with their lives.

Move on with his life.

Walk away.

It was the right thing to do; he knew it was, and it was what Hannah wanted.

That didn't mean it was going to be easy.

CHAPTER
Two

December 19th
9:26 A.M.

"Do we have anything from ERT?" Tom asked Chloe as they sat down at their desks.

"No fingerprints. We do have the bullet the doctors removed from Jeff Shields in the emergency room. ERT is running it through ballistics. Hopefully we'll get a match."

The armed robbers hadn't fired any shots at the scenes of any of the other robberies, so there was no possibility of linking the crimes that way, but if they got a hit to a particular gun then they might be able to find the shooter. "No fibers or DNA or anything?" he asked. He wanted something that would conclusively prove the robbery at Hannah's store *was* related to the others. He just didn't know what that conclusive evidence would be. The Evidence Response Team Unit had scoured the scenes of all four of the previous robberies and come up with no forensic evidence. How could he find a link between the four other crimes and the one at Hannah's store when they had no forensics and no descriptions of the robbers?

"Nothing. I'm sorry, Tom. I know you want to confirm that the same men committed the other robberies and the one at your . . . uh . . . *friend's* store," Chloe finished, arching a perfectly sculpted brow at him.

He just nodded. He didn't want to discuss Hannah with his partner. Or with anyone else. He just wanted to solve this case, get some closure, and move on with his life.

"Who is she?" Chloe asked. His partner wasn't one for tact and was clearly choosing to ignore the blatant signals he was giving that he didn't want to talk about it.

"My ex-wife," he replied. If he refused to answer, it would only further pique her curiosity.

"I didn't know you were married. Why did you two split up?"

"Chloe," he reprimanded.

"What?" she asked, brown eyes all wide and innocent. "We only just became partners, I'm just getting to know you."

Working with Chloe Luckman was going to be interesting, if nothing else. She was a recent graduate from the academy. She was full of enthusiasm and zeal for her job. She was smart and strong, and just like him, she paid attention to details. He liked her; he just didn't want to discuss his failed marriage with her.

Her face softened. "She was most stressed out by the gun. Has she been held at gunpoint before?"

He may as well just tell her. She obviously wasn't going to give up, and it wasn't like she couldn't find the information out on her own anyway. Besides, if he was right and the robbery at Hannah's store was committed by a different set of perpetrators than the others, then it might even end up being relevant to the case.

"Hannah was raped," he told her. He hated that word. Hated the way it felt in his mouth, hated the images it conjured up in his mind, hated what it had done to the woman he loved.

"Oh, Tom, I'm so sorry." Chloe's eyes filled with sympathy.

"Hannah has been through enough. I want to make sure that if this has anything to do with her and not just the jewelry that we get those men off the street before they try to hurt her again."

"You really think it's not related?"

"I don't know. It just feels different, and I want to be sure. And not just because it's Hannah. If we're dealing with two different sets of perpetrators, we need to get them both off the streets."

"Okay, well let's go back to the first robbery."

"November twenty-first, around 2:00 P.M., three armed men wearing jeans, black hoodies, and clown masks enter a small jewelry store in a quiet strip mall. Inside there were two employees and three customers. A middle-aged couple looking for an engagement ring, and an older woman looking for a gift for her granddaughter's sixteenth birthday. They came in, demanded jewelry, smashed a few of the glass cases, grabbed what they could and ran. In and out in under two minutes. No one was hurt. They didn't ask for codes to the safe. They just took what was accessible."

"Second robbery was similar," Chloe said. "Exactly one week later, on November twenty-eighth, 1:00 P.M., another strip mall jewelry store. Again, three men, dressed the same, armed with guns, enter the store, where there are five employees and six customers. They demand jewelry, smash the glass cases, and run off with whatever they could grab. Witnesses say they weren't in there any longer than two or three minutes. They didn't ask for codes or entry to the safe."

"Third one occurred a week later once again, December fifth; they hit at midday. Same MO as the others; this time there are four employees and only one customer. Fourth one was one week later on the twelfth. Three employees, eight customers, they struck at three in the afternoon. In none of those four robberies do they ask for anything else other than what they can easily grab."

"Maybe they built up enough confidence after the first four and were ready to escalate things," Chloe said.

"Maybe," he nodded. "Times of day were different, too. The other crimes were committed in the early afternoon. The one at Hannah's was at night, after the store was already closed."

"Again, that could fit in with the escalation. It's easier to try and get the more expensive stuff from the safe when there are less people there."

"Maybe," he acknowledged again. "I agree, the differences in time of day and what they're after could just be an escalation related to gaining confidence and moving on to bigger things. But they struck a day early. If they kept with their pattern, they should have robbed their next store on the nineteenth, not the eighteenth."

"Maybe something was going to prevent them from hitting a store today," Chloe countered. "Or maybe they realized it made them too predictable. If they kept going with the same day, then we were going to catch them. This way they make it more difficult, and we don't know when they're going to strike."

"The men who attacked Hannah didn't wear clown masks. They wore balaclavas," he moved on to his next argument.

"Could be the clown masks got lost or broken, or they just changed their minds and decided to go with something different."

"We can explain away every difference between the robberies except one."

"There were only two people who robbed Hannah's store," Chloe said.

"Exactly."

"One could be sick," his partner suggested. "Or otherwise occupied."

"If you're running a robbery ring, you only hit a store when you can all do it. If one of them was sick, they would have waited until today; this is when they were supposed to strike. A group of three men robbed stores coming away with only a couple of thousand dollars' worth of stolen jewelry. A group of two men robbed Hannah's store, attempting to walk away with millions."

"What are the odds there are two separate gangs hitting jewelry stores in the same city at the same time?"

"Not very high," he answered Chloe's rhetorical question.

"Maybe the hit on Hannah's store was someone hoping to take advantage of the other robberies. They knew we were looking at a gang of robbers, and they could swoop in, make it out with millions in stolen jewels, then disappear, all the while we think we're looking for someone else."

"I suppose," Tom agreed. It was a viable possibility and certainly preferable to the alternative, that Hannah was the intended target.

"Last night's was the only one that turned violent. But was it because it was just different men who wanted something different, or because they had always intended to turn things violent?"

"There's no way to know that."

"No, there's not. If the robbery at Hannah's store was committed by different men, then who? And why? Do you know of anyone that would want to hurt her?"

"There's no one who would want to hurt her," he replied adamantly. Hannah was stubborn, but so sweet, he couldn't imagine her making any enemies even if she tried.

"What about the man who raped her?"

"Prison," he replied shortly.

"Let's say you're right, and it was someone else. Do we know for sure she was the target? After all, it was Jeff Shields who was shot."

"If Jeff was the target, then why would they shoot him at Hannah's store? If someone was after him, then there were plenty of other places they could have shot him."

"If Hannah was the target, then why didn't they shoot *her*?"

"I don't know."

"If there *was* an ulterior motive to this robbery, then I think we should be looking at Jeff and not Hannah."

"We will look at Jeff. When his doctors clear him, we'll interview him and see if there's anyone who might want to hurt him by staging a robbery."

"Why would we think it was staged as a robbery at all? I mean, they broke in, they smashed the glass cases and took what they could, they try to get the code for the safe so they can take even more with them. Then, when they can't get what they came for, they turn violent to try to get it. Why would we look at this as anything other than a robbery gone wrong?"

"Because we want to look at all the possibilities," he replied, or rather, lied. Tom couldn't explain why he thought this was not just an ordinary robbery. "Two different groups of men committed these crimes, and we have to look at the motivations. We don't have any forensics yet, so we need to keep ourselves open to everything."

"I agree. We *do* have to keep ourselves open to everything. Including to the possibility that it's just coincidence that there are two separate groups of robbers operating at the same time. And just because it does look like two different groups of perpetrators, that doesn't mean this has anything to do with Hannah. I think you're letting what happened to her and who she is to you cloud your judgment."

Logic told him Chloe was right.

There was nothing to suggest that this was anything more than a random robbery.

So why couldn't he shake the feeling that it was something more?

Was he just imagining things because it involved Hannah? Was he just after a reason to spend more time around her? Was he just after a scenario where this time he could save her?

Or was Hannah really in danger?

∿

10:13 A.M.

It felt weird walking back in here.

She didn't want to be here.

She wanted to never come back here again.

But Hannah wouldn't do that. She would *never* run away from things that scared her, no matter how tempting that may seem at times. It just wasn't who she was. She faced her problems, she tried to work through them, she tried to make the best of even the worst of situations. She had done it before, and she would do it again.

What had happened here at her store wouldn't destroy her.

And it wouldn't make her go back to that dark place.

She had worked so hard to get out of the dark and claw her way back to the light, or even the dull, she couldn't go back there. Not under any circumstances. So, she had no choice but to process the robbery, deal with it as best she could, and move on.

Dwelling on the gun-wielding robbers wasn't going to be productive, and today was all about productivity. She had a lot of work to do. The cops and crime scene unit were finished in the store, and since, including today, there were only six shopping days left until Christmas, she had to get this place cleaned up so she could open tomorrow.

Her store was one big mess. There were glass shards all over the floor from where the robbers had smashed all the glass cases. She didn't remember hearing them do that, but obviously they had because the glass was everywhere and she could see some of her stock was missing. What they hadn't grabbed was half still in the broken counters and half littered throughout the glass. The seven-foot Christmas tree that had been in the corner was lying on its side, fairy lights and tinsel tangled on the floor around it, and shattered decorations were scattered about. There was fingerprint powder everywhere from the crime scene unit, and she knew that through the door into her workroom, there was still the giant puddle of Jeff's blood.

Tears threatened to swamp her.

She loved her store, but now being here was torture. Her mind wanted to keep replaying last night's events over and over on a loop until it sent her insane.

"Deep breaths," she ordered herself out loud. "Deep breaths."

Following her own instructions, Hannah cleared her mind of everything else and focused on simply inhaling air through her nose and letting it whoosh out through her mouth.

When she felt marginally calmer, she faced her store.

She could do this.

One step at a time, just like always.

First thing she had to do was collect up all her inventory that have been left strewn about and put it in the safe where she could go through it later and make a list of everything that had been taken.

Unable to face the workroom and all the blood, for now she just left everything in a box by the door.

Once that was taken care of she couldn't put off going through into the rest of the store any longer. She needed a broom to sweep up the glass and something to wipe down all the powder.

With another steadying breath, she opened the door, and without letting herself pause and over think things, she stepped through it. Her breathing quickened, and she began to shake. Hannah had to sternly remind herself that the gun was no longer in here and that Jeff was going to be okay.

This was silly.

She was going to have to do something about the gun phobia. She'd never really worried about it before because it wasn't like she came into contact with guns very often. Or ever. Last night had been the first one she had seen since the night of her assault.

But her phobia had nearly gotten her and her employees killed.

It was time to face that fear and find a way to conquer it. After Christmas, she would call her therapist and see about maybe trying some exposure therapy to work through her gun issues.

Feeling better now that she had decided to take action on overcoming her phobia, Hannah headed to the cupboard in the corner and collected cleaning supplies. For the next hour or so she was so immersed in her tasks that the fear and horror of the robbery began to fade, and the store began to feel more like it used to.

Finally, she paused and stretched her back.

There was only one task left.

The blood.

She'd been putting it off because the guilt that swamped her whenever she looked at it was almost crushing.

How could she ever face Jeff again? He had tried to save her from being shot and gotten himself shot instead.

She sucked her bottom lip in and chewed on it, forcing back the tears that burned the backs of her eyes.

Jeff was going to be okay. She just had to keep reminding herself of that, as many times as it took for it to sink in.

Filling a bucket with water, she sank down on her knees and soaked the cloth, ready to begin scrubbing, but she just couldn't. She felt so overwhelmed. It had been a long time since she felt this way. And part of it was seeing Tom again. That brought up memories from her rape, which had eventually led to their divorce.

The towel Tom had used to clean her up last night still lay discarded, right where she'd been sitting. Hannah picked it up and studied it as though it held the answers to the questions swirling around inside her head.

She was so confused about Tom.

She had never been so hurt in her life than when he had told her he was leaving. After everything they had been through, she'd thought they would be together forever.

But he'd seen things differently.

He had seen her as a helpless victim, and neither of them had been able to work around that perception.

Was she a victim?

Yes.

Was she helpless?

Never.

While she wanted to regain the sense of strength and confidence and stability that had been ripped away from her, Tom wanted to hold her in his arms and rock her and promise her that everything would be okay.

But being coddled didn't help her.

And being told everything would be okay certainly didn't help.

She'd been brutally raped. How could anything ever be okay again?

Just because things couldn't be okay didn't mean they couldn't get better. She had worked *so* hard to rebuild her life. She had gone to the victims' support group and talked with other survivors of sexual assault about how they were coping. She had seen her therapist religiously and worked diligently on everything the woman had asked her to do. She had taken her medication even though the idea of taking it left her a little uneasy. And she had kept going with all the regular things she did in her life—work, gym, shopping, chores, eating out, seeing friends— when most days all she wanted to do was curl up in bed and cry.

She had fought for her life because she didn't want her rape to define her.

Not that it had been easy.

And it really hadn't.

It had been hell.

Almost as bad as enduring the assault itself.

She'd had nightmares. Regularly waking several times a night screaming or drenched in an ice cold sweat, she'd had flashbacks to the assault. She started becoming hypervigilant of her surroundings, constantly checking everyone who was around her and trying to judge whether they could be a threat or not. She started to obsessively check things like whether every door and window in the house was locked before she went to bed, sometimes spending close to an hour just circling the house checking them repeatedly.

With time, she had learned to manage all those things. The fear was still there, like a distant shadow hovering in the recesses of her mind. The compulsion to vigilantly study her surroundings and to check and recheck her home each night was always there. Hannah knew those things would never leave her, but so long as she could manage them, then she felt like she had overcome what had happened to her.

She just wished that Tom had seen it the same way.

He had wanted to fix everything for her, and what had happened couldn't be fixed. It could only be treated.

He had been supportive of her seeing a therapist and comforted her more nights than she could count when nightmares had plagued her. But he couldn't shake the need to save her.

She hadn't needed a savior; all she'd needed was her husband.

But he had walked away.

And she had let him.

Not because it was easy, but because letting him go was what was best for him.

Hannah couldn't blame him for leaving. Three years ago, when everything had been so fresh, she had been such a mess. They had both known she had a long road ahead of her, and she couldn't really fault him for choosing not to walk it with her.

And she knew that he had been suffering, too. She had asked him several times to come and see a therapist with her, or to go on his own if he preferred, but he hadn't been ready to admit that he needed it. Tom couldn't accept that what had happened had happened to both of them, and that both of them needed time to heal.

She wasn't angry with Tom for walking away from their marriage; it just hurt. A lot. So much that she wasn't sure she could ever move past it. She still loved him. Probably always would. But sometimes love wasn't enough. She hadn't thought that those feelings would ever be stirred up again. They were divorced. She had her life; he had his. There was no reason for their lives to intersect.

Until yesterday.

Now, for the next little while at least, Tom was back in her life.

He was an added complication when she really didn't need one.

She scrunched her eyes closed and wished she could make the last twenty-four hours so they never happened.

Instead, when she opened her eyes, she saw Tom standing in front of her.

~

11:47 A.M.

Her eyes, which today were a desolate blue gray like the ocean on a winter's day, widened in surprise when she opened them to see him standing there. "Tom."

"You shouldn't be here on your own." He said the words without thinking, and only because he hated to see Hannah suffer. And he knew being here cleaning up the mess from last night's robbery would make her suffer.

Immediately, her eyes darkened and she scowled at him. "I'm not a child, I can do things myself. I don't need someone to come in here and clean up for me. There are only a few days left until Christmas, and I want to make the most of them." With that, she sloshed the towel in her hands into the bucket of water at her side, sending droplets splashing all over the place, and began to scrub the floor.

"I never said you were a child, Hannah," he said softly. He didn't know why she got so crazy every time he expressed concern.

"You always treat me like one. Like I'm helpless and useless and couldn't possibly be able to cope all on my own."

He had never once thought of Hannah as any of those things. Quite the opposite, in fact. He thought she was smart and strong, more resilient than he could ever imagine being. "I'm sorry if I gave you that impression, but I don't think you're helpless and useless. I never thought that."

Hannah merely harrumphed and continued scrubbing vigorously at the bloodstain on the floor.

For a moment, all Tom could do was stare at it.

What if Jeff Shields hadn't come in when he had? Then it wouldn't be his blood spattered all over the floor and walls. It would be Hannah's.

To know that she had come so close to being shot choked him up in a way that made him know that no matter how much time passed or how much distance there was between them, part of him would always love Hannah.

Tom went to her, crouched at her side, and put his hands over hers, stilling them. "I never thought you were incapable of coping on your own. I don't know why you'd even think that."

"You don't know why I would think that?" she repeated incredulously. "Maybe because after the attack you hovered over me constantly, wanting to do everything for me, acting like you could just wipe it all away by pretending it never happened. Well, it happened, Tom. It happened."

"I know it happened. I was there."

"Yeah, you were. So, maybe instead of trying to coddle me, you should have encouraged me to get strong again."

"I did."

"You didn't. You treated me like a victim."

He bit his tongue to keep from reminding her that she *had* been a victim. "I don't know why you acted like me wanting to be there for you was such a bad thing. You pushed me away every chance you got."

"I never pushed you away."

"That was all you did." Sometimes it felt like they had lived in two completely different worlds after the assault.

"Wanting to do things for myself wasn't pushing you away."

"It was like you didn't want me around anymore."

"*You're* the one who walked away, not me."

"I walked away because it was what you wanted."

"How did you know it was what I wanted? Did you ask me? No, you didn't. You just assumed that and walked out the door, never looking back."

"You shut me out at every opportunity, Hannah."

"You were smothering me. You treated me like if you didn't hover at my side every second I was going to shatter into a million pieces. You wanted to focus on me so you didn't have to admit that you were struggling every bit as much as I was. You're not superman, Tom, and I didn't need you to be. I just wanted you to be you. But you wouldn't do that. Either I let you take care of me or nothing. Well what if I wanted to take care of you, too? We should have been taking care of each other."

He didn't know what to say to that.

Was she right?

Had he been so stubborn that it was either his way or no way?

He had honestly thought that Hannah hadn't wanted him around anymore. That she had chosen to shut herself off and deal with what had happened by herself—without him. But obviously she saw things differently.

"I'm not broken, Tom. I would never let those men win and break me. Only you didn't see it that way. You saw me as a project to fix. Not as a human being anymore. Not as your wife anymore." Tears shimmered in her eyes, making them bluer. "You threw our marriage away because you didn't support me getting better."

How could she even think that? Didn't support her getting better? That was ridiculous. He would have done anything to help Hannah get through what had happened. "I don't know why you say such absurd stuff."

"Absurd was throwing away a marriage because you were too stubborn to admit you needed help, too."

"That's not what happened."

"Yes, it was."

"No, it wasn't."

"Yes, it was."

"No, it wasn't."

"Yes, it was!"

"You're impossible," he huffed, releasing her hand and standing, stalking across the room, aggravated. Why did she have to argue about everything? Why couldn't the two of them be in the same room together without things disintegrating into childish bickering?

"Well, there's the door; feel free to use it." She shrugged with a perfect air of disinterest he would have believed if he didn't know her so well. The slight tremor that rippled through her told the story of how her emotions were in disarray.

The tremor reminded him of how badly she'd been shaking when he'd arrived here last night.

Which reminded him of the robbery and just why he'd come looking for her.

Getting distracted with arguing wasn't helpful right now. He had a job to do. So long as he kept reminding himself that this was just a job, and that he could walk away again once it was complete, he should be able to get through it without endless quarreling.

Hannah's life was nothing to mess with, and he would take her frustrated lashing out so long as it kept her safe.

Just a job.

If he had to remind himself of that a hundred times a day, he would.

Just a job.

He returned to her side, picked up a towel, and began to help her clean the floor.

"I thought you were leaving."

"For once, just let me help you without arguing. You don't have to do everything on your own all the time."

She said nothing, and for a while they worked in silence.

When they were done, he took the bucket and emptied it out in the bathroom. When he came back into the workroom, Hannah was sitting on the floor, leaning against the wall, her head tipped back and her eyes closed.

"Why are you here, Tom?" she asked without opening her eyes.

"Because I'm worried about you."

"I'll be fine."

"I know you will. But something feels different about the robbery at your store."

That prompted her to open her eyes and look at him. "Different, how?" she asked suspiciously.

"I'm not convinced it was committed by the same people who committed the others."

"Why wouldn't it be?" Hannah looked confused.

"There are some differences. The main one being that a gang of three armed men robbed the other stores, and only two armed men held up you and your employees."

"Maybe one just couldn't be there last night," she countered.

"Maybe. But I don't think it's related."

"So, there're two groups of thieves looking to make a quick buck robbing jewelry stores this Christmas?" She closed her eyes again, and wearily rested her head back against the wall.

"Maybe."

Her head snapped up. "What do you mean *maybe*? What else could it be?"

"I don't know," he answered honestly. Chloe was right, he had to make sure he wasn't seeing monsters where there weren't any just because of his history with Hannah.

"Tom?"

"It probably is just two gangs of thieves committing robberies."

"But?" she prompted.

"But I just want you to be careful, in case it's something else."

"Something else like you think this could be personal?"

"Could it be?" he asked.

"I don't think so."

"You don't think so?" He wanted something much more concrete than that. He wanted Hannah to give him an absolute denial that the robbery being anything more than a random robbery was out of the question.

"Who would want to target me through my store? There's no one. No one who would want to hurt me. If it's not random, maybe it's Jeff or Vincent they were really interested in."

"Do you think it could be?"

"I don't think so. Not Jeff. And Vincent is just the son of a friend who needed a job. I don't know much about him, but I can't imagine robbing my store would be a good way to hurt him if someone wanted to. Do you really think this could be more than just a random robbery?"

Fear crept into her face, and he wanted to say whatever it took to wipe it away. Instead, he said, "I can't discount the possibility."

"Oh." Her face fell, and she began to chew on her lower lip, a sure sign she was stressed and scared but trying not to show it.

"I don't want you to worry. I'll figure it out," he assured her.

"Yeah, you will," she said, a hint of sadness in her tone.

The sadness hit him harder than the fear. It was like no matter what he did, he caused her pain.

Just a job, he reminded himself, just a job.

When it was over, he could walk away just like he'd done before, then he would never hurt Hannah again.

3:19 P.M.

"Yes, ma'am, we can certainly call another store and see if they have this bangle in white gold." Chloe smiled at the woman in front of her.

"And what about this one?" The woman pointed at another bracelet in the glass case. "Can I try it on, please?"

"Of course."

As she opened the cabinet, Chloe let her mind wander. She really hoped this plan worked. They had to get these armed robbers off the street. Today was the day the gang usually hit so they were hoping that despite last night's change in plans, they went back to their usual schedule and hit again. They had agents in all the stores they thought were viable targets, playing the roles of both employees and customers.

She had enthusiastically volunteered to take part. She didn't want to sit on the sidelines in one of the vans watching the streets outside the stores to keep watch for anyone who might be the men they were after. She wanted to be right in the thick of things.

Being an FBI agent was her dream job.

Ever since she was ten, Chloe had known this was what she wanted to do with her life. What she was *meant* to do with her life. That day had set the whole course of her life into motion, and now she was finally living her dream. She was here, on only her second case, working as a decoy, and anxiously hoping that if the robbers hit today, that it would be this store.

Nervous butterflies fluttered in her stomach. As much as she wanted to be here, and as much as she didn't think that the men they were looking for were going to hurt her or anyone else, adrenalin was still flying through her system.

Chloe agreed with her partner that it looked like they were after two different sets of criminals.

One that had committed the first four robberies. They'd gotten away with minimal jewelry and hadn't done more than threaten customers and employees. They hadn't physically hurt anyone, and they seemed to just get in and out and away as quickly as possible by grabbing whatever they could get their hands on in the glass showcases. They didn't want to risk waiting until a silent alarm brought cops running.

And one who'd tried to play it big but ended up walking away with next to nothing.

She might agree with Tom on that, but she didn't agree that the robbery at his ex's store was anything but a robbery. Sure, two robberies by two different perpetrators so close together was unusual, but it certainly wasn't out of the realm of possibility.

Although Chloe understood why her partner saw it differently. His judgment was clouded by his personal connection to the victim. She was intrigued by Tom's past with Hannah, but was resisting the urge to go and look up the woman's case to find out the details. She liked working with Tom, and she thought she could learn a lot from him, but not if she broke trust between them. They needed to trust one another; their lives might one day depend on it. Hopefully, once she and Tom got to know each other better, he would tell her about what had happened with his ex-wife himself.

A chime broke her train of thought, and her gaze snapped to the store's door, half expecting to see three men in clown masks wielding guns come storming in.

Instead, it was a couple. A man and woman who were off-duty cops at the local precinct and playing the parts of a young couple choosing an engagement ring. While Chloe continued to deal with the cop pretending to be interested in a new gold and sapphire bracelet, a man—another special agent—went to show engagement rings to the couple.

This was exactly how she had imagined her job.

Being right in the thick of things.

She could get used to this buzz.

The fun of lying in wait to catch her prey.

The power rush knowing that the robbers were going to walk right into a perfectly crafted trap.

She didn't want to give this up for anything.

And yet . . .

There was a chance she would have to.

At least for a while.

Her hand strayed to her stomach where her baby was growing.

Getting pregnant had been a mistake. Well, not a mistake; more like a severe case of bad timing. She and her boyfriend had been together for almost two years, but she had just graduated from the FBI academy and started her dream job. Having to take time off now was not the optimum.

No one knew yet. She was only a month or so along, so she had a little bit of time before she had to start telling people. She hadn't even told her boyfriend. She was on the pill, so it was going to come as a major shock to him. It had come as a major shock to *her*. It was the last thing she'd been expecting.

Now she didn't know what to do.

She loved her job and didn't want to have to give it up, even just for a few months. Once she got too far along, she would be relegated to a desk. That was her worst nightmare. She wanted to be out in the field, catching bad guys and helping people, not sitting in an office. And then when the baby came, it would be maternity leave, but she didn't want to spend her days stuck in the house changing diapers and preparing bottles.

But the only way to avoid both was dramatic and not something she even wanted to consider, although . . .

"Chloe."

She started at her partner's voice, and turned, expecting to see him standing behind her.

Then she remembered she was wearing an earpiece and her partner was in a van parked outside the store.

Resisting the urge to answer him, she smiled at the woman in front of her and set out another bracelet for her to try on.

"Three men approaching. One minute out. Could be our guys."

Adrenalin surged.

This was it.

The first time she was ever going to be in a potentially dangerous situation. Chloe clung to her training. It had all boiled down to this one moment.

The door swung open.

Three men, with guns drawn and wearing clown masks, entered.

No one made a move yet.

They wanted to let the men make the first move, so there could be no doubt when this went to court that their intentions had been to rob the store. They didn't want the men arguing that it had just been some prank or some other ridiculous defense.

"No one move," one ordered, crossing to the nearest counter, which just so happened to be the one she was standing behind.

Her stomach in knots, it took every ounce of self-restraint she possessed not to pull out her gun and badge and order the men down on the ground.

While one of the men remained at the door, the other two started to smash the glass cabinets and grab whatever they could get their hands on, stuffing it into bags.

In her earpiece, she heard someone count down.

"Three, two, one."

At one, the officers who were waiting out of sight in the back room and the cops, including her partner, who were surrounding the building, all burst out, guns drawn.

"Down, down, down, on your knees!"

As orders were shouted out, the three men panicked.

Two obviously weighed up their options and decided the smartest course of action was to comply, discarding their weapons and dropping to the floor.

The third—the one standing just in front of her—remained on his feet.

She was about to order him down again, when suddenly he flew over the counter and pressed his gun to her head. His arm across her chest pinned her firmly against him.

He yelled something to the rest of the cops, something she didn't hear but assumed was a threat that if they did anything he would blow her brains out.

There was no way Chloe was being the human shield this man used to walk out of here. Besides, she could handle this. She didn't need to wait for the others to try to talk him down.

When he started to pull her backward toward the office space at the back, she placed her hands on his forearm and pulled it a little farther from her neck so she could make her move. She slammed her head back, connecting squarely with the man's nose, then without stopping, she lifted her foot and brought it down firmly on his. Then she dropped one hand and hit his groin, then rammed her elbow into his ribs and up into his jaw, before twisting out of his grip.

Caught off guard, he released her, and as she moved herself out of reach, he lashed out with his fist and connected firmly with her stomach.

As pain radiated out across her body, everything else but her baby fled from her mind.

~

3:52 P.M.

Images of Hannah with a gun held at her head flashed through his mind as one of the armed robbers launched across the glass cabinets and wrapped an arm around his partner, yanking her against his chest and shoving his gun to her temple.

Tom had to block those memories out so he could focus.

While a couple of officers cuffed the two other robbers, the rest of the agents and officers in the room focused on the hostage situation.

"Put your guns down or I shoot her," the masked man screamed.

Not a single cop lowered their weapon.

You didn't have to be able to see the man's face to know that he was panicked. He was in way over his head. What he had thought was going to be a simple grab-and-run robbery had suddenly escalated, and now he didn't know what to do. Tom prayed he played it smart.

"You're not walking out of this building except in handcuffs," he told the man, pleased when his voice came out strong and calm despite the near deafening sound of his pulse thumping in his ears.

The man inched his way backward toward the door that led through to the office and then out onto the street. "I'm not going back to prison."

And no one in this room was letting him walk out of it holding an FBI special agent as a human shield.

Which only left death.

Tom hoped the man was smart enough not to take the suicide by cop route.

"Think about what you're doing," he urged the man who didn't sound much older than a kid. "So far, you haven't hurt anyone. You want to keep it that way. Release the woman and put your weapon down," he ordered.

"No. No prison." The kid sounded on the verge of tears.

Before Tom could say more, Chloe suddenly flung her head back into the man's face and executed a self-defense move to free herself from the robber's grip.

Startled, the man released her, but as she twisted away, he managed to get in a blow to her abdomen.

Several people lunged at the man, tackling him to the ground, while Tom darted forward, hooked an arm across Chloe's chest and dragged her out of reach.

Was his partner insane?

What had possessed her to do that?

She could have gotten herself killed.

They would have talked the man down.

As he released her, Chloe rolled into a ball, her arms wrapped around her stomach. How badly was she hurt?

"I need medics," he yelled over his shoulder. "Chloe," he gently tugged on her shoulders until she lifted her head.

Her eyes had been closed but she opened them to stare up at him. "I'm pregnant. My baby."

Pregnant?

Chloe was pregnant?

If he'd known that, he would never have allowed her to take part in the sting. He would have made sure she was safely in the van beside him. He was her supervising officer and he was responsible for her safety. Not only could she have been killed or seriously injured, but her unborn baby could have, as well.

"He hit my stomach, am I bleeding? What if he hurt the baby?" Tears were brimming in her brown eyes, and her bottom lip wobbled.

"How far along are you?"

"A month."

Tom relaxed. "Then the baby should be fine. In the first trimester, the uterus isn't exposed. It's still protected by the pelvis, the chances of a blow to your stomach harming the fetus are low."

"How do you know that?" she asked warily.

"Sister's an OB-GYN," he replied. He knew more about pregnancies and childbirth than most fathers with several kids.

"You're sure?"

"Positive, but we'll get you checked out to confirm that the baby is okay."

Chloe relaxed and sank back against the floor, releasing the death grip she'd had on her stomach. He suspected she had been more afraid than she had been in pain.

As his partner relaxed, Tom felt his blood pressure rise.

She had endangered herself and her child. While her little self-defense stunt had worked, it could just as easily not have.

"Did they get him?" Chloe sat up and turned her attention to where the man who'd held her at gunpoint was being cuffed and dragged to his feet. Someone had removed his mask, and she said, "He looks so young. Probably still a teenager."

How could she act like nothing had happened?

If she had been seriously hurt or killed, or if she had miscarried her baby, he would never have forgiven himself for putting her in a poten-tially dangerous situation.

His fear and guilt channeled themselves into anger. "What were you thinking? You don't ever do something that reckless! What if his finger had tightened on the trigger when you hit him? He would have fired. The bullet would have gone straight through that thick head of yours. If you hadn't been so stubborn and too busy thinking that you're bullet-proof, you could have waited while we talked him down and got you safely away from him."

Chloe's eyes grew wide. "Everything worked out fine."

But it might not have.

He remembered back when he had first started his career in the FBI. He had been just like Chloe—young, enthusiastic, eager, bulletproof. Back then everything had seemed so simple. Catch the bad guys. That was all he'd wanted to do, and he had been prepared to do whatever it took to do it.

Then *that night* had happened, and his life had changed.

In one instant, he had learned that sometimes the bad guys won.

When he had watched his wife be gang raped, believing that when they were finished torturing her they were going to kill her and then him, his world had ceased to be simple.

Now he was careful, weighing the risks and the pros and cons of every situation before making a move. Now he didn't take unnecessary risks. He knew just how fragile life truly was.

One day, Chloe would learn that, too.

He just prayed it wasn't in such a tragic way as he had learned the lesson.

"I don't know why you're being so melodramatic." His partner was looking at him like he'd suddenly grown two heads. "I thought the purpose of learning those self-defense skills was to use them in situations such as someone holding a gun to your head. We all know no one was letting him walk out of here with me. And no one really wanted to shoot him. He's just a kid, and he most likely never physically hurt anyone. I saved anyone from having to shoot him. Everything worked out fine, Tom; there's no need to stress."

Stress was a natural part of his life now.

Born that night, it grew as he watched Hannah struggle to deal with what had happened to her. Now it was as much a part of him as breathing.

Chloe's blasé attitude didn't fool him. He saw the flicker of fear in her eyes. No one could have a gun held to their head and not be at least a little moved by the vivid confrontation of their own mortality. Hopefully that was as close as she ever got to thinking she would die until she was an old woman who had lived her life to the fullest.

Still, Chloe seemed to be holding it together. She was calm and in control, although he suspected a lot of that was keeping up appearances in front of their colleagues. But she was right; she was fine, uninjured, although he would make sure paramedics checked her out to determine she and her baby were okay.

He needed to calm himself down.

This situation with Hannah had him more stressed out than usual.

Now, at least, they could get some answers. They had the robbers, and once they interviewed them, they'd be able to confirm that these three kids had not held his ex at gunpoint and shot her employee. Then, once they knew that, they could start going through Hannah's life and those of the two men there with her that night, to see whether any of them could be the target.

Tom already knew the answer, though. He felt it in his bones. This was about Hannah, and he would do whatever it took to make sure she didn't end up with another gun held at her head.

CHAPTER
Three

December 20th
8:33 A.M.

"How're you doing this morning?" Tom asked Chloe as she set her bag down on her desk.

"I'm fine." She gave him a small frown as she unwound her scarf and shrugged out of her coat.

"No nightmares?"

"No."

"Did you have trouble sleeping?"

"No."

"Any issues with coming to work this morning?"

"No, Tom." She sounded exasperated.

"Did you make an appointment to see the department counselor?" he asked, undaunted by Chloe's unwillingness to talk about what had happened yesterday.

"Yes, I did. Now, stop grilling me. It's none of your business. I'm not your ex."

"No, you're not," he agreed calmly, refusing to be baited into a conversation about Hannah. "You're my partner. The person I have to trust to have my back. I'm not grilling you to annoy you. I'm grilling you because I care."

He believed that Chloe had the potential to be an amazing agent. She was smart, and her attention to detail rivaled his own. She was also caring and compassionate, and she wanted to make a difference. He was looking forward to getting to know her better and to work with her.

But she also had the potential to get herself hurt. She wanted her sole focus to be the end game, but if she didn't pay attention to how she got there, she was a risk to herself and everyone around her. She couldn't be reckless. She had to be smart—always.

Chloe's annoyed face softened. "You're right, I'm sorry. Thank you for caring. And you're right, we do have to trust each other. Yesterday I did what I thought was right. Maybe I should have waited for you guys to talk him down. Maybe that was the safer option, I'm not sure, but I *am* sorry that it stressed you."

Tom nodded. His partner didn't get how important it was to play things safe yet, but one day she would. This was only her second case. Everything was still new and fresh for her. And maybe he had overreacted a little yesterday. He *was* on edge the last few days because of seeing Hannah again, particularly under these circumstances.

He knew he had a reputation for paying obsessive attention to the details in everything he did, and he also knew that that reputation had developed after Hannah's assault. That night had changed both of them. And maybe if he'd been paying better attention to things that night, it would never have happened. He wouldn't make that mistake again, but he also knew he couldn't visit his issues on his partner.

"I just want you to be safe, Chloe. Particularly now that you have someone who's counting on you."

"I won't take unnecessary risks," she assured him.

He hoped that was true. "You ready to interview Warren Maloney?"

Warren Maloney was the nineteen-year-old kid who'd held a gun to Chloe's head yesterday afternoon. The other two men were his seventeen-year-old brother and an eighteen-year-old cousin. Yesterday, the kids had gone through the booking process and now they were able to interview the gang's ringleader. Tom had been on pins and needles all night, anxious for confirmation that these three kids didn't hold up Hannah's store.

"Yep," Chloe nodded eagerly.

"We want information about the robberies," he reminded her, "not about what happened yesterday."

"I know," she assured him.

Tom held back a small smile. Chloe's passion and zeal were quite endearing. He just hoped she learned to channel them appropriately and use them to her advantage.

"Good morning, Mr. Maloney," he said as they entered the interview room where Warren and his lawyer were waiting for them.

The young man just glared at them. Warren Maloney was an angry kid. Expelled from school at the age of fourteen after getting into several fights, he started stealing cars. At the age of fifteen, he did his first stint in a juvenile detention facility. When he came out, he went straight back to stealing cars, this time carjacking people at gunpoint. After the last prison stint, he had apparently decided to ditch cars and try robbing jewelry stores instead. Warren was tall and thin with a baby face that made him look no older than about thirteen. Until you looked into his eyes, which were ice blue and cold and weathered as though he'd lived a hundred years already.

"You're facing serious charges, Mr. Maloney," Tom continued. "Multiple counts of armed robbery, assault of a federal agent. There's no denying the charges, claiming it wasn't you. No excuses. There are a dozen cops and agents who saw you do it."

"I didn't hurt her," Warren said sullenly, his bushy eyebrows knitting together.

"You held a gun to her head."

"I ain't going back to prison." Warren's blue eyes stared defiantly.

"You most certainly are."

"Am not." Warren turned to his public defender to seek support.

"They have you for this robbery and the assault on the agent." The middle-aged lawyer flicked his hand in Chloe's direction. "Getting off on any of those charges would be unlikely. The other robberies—they don't really have anything to connect them to you."

"Who said there were others?" Warren aimed for nonchalance but looked more nervous than anything else.

"We know there were others. Three men in clown masks, brandishing guns held up four other jewelry stores," Chloe said. "We know that. That's not what we want to talk to you about."

"Your brother doesn't have a criminal record." Tom changed the subject.

"Did you have to talk him into committing the robberies with you?" Chloe asked.

"He's a good kid. Had his whole life ahead of him. He was doing well in school. He could have gone to college and with hard work, been anything he wanted to be, done anything he wanted to do."

"How did you convince him to throw it all away?"

"Your cousin is a drug addict, right? Is that how you convinced him to help you?"

"He probably agreed fairly readily. Anything to make a quick buck."

"What did you do with the jewelry?"

"Did you pawn it?"

"Did you sell it online?"

"Did you sell it on the black market?"

"Between the two robberies you got away with, close to twenty-thousand-dollars'-worth of jewelry. Not bad for less than ten minutes' work."

"What was your long-term goal? Did you want the money to start over or to do something with, or did you just want to scare some people?"

"Who fired the shot that hit Jeff Shields?" Tom asked.

Warren Maloney's head had been snapping backward and forward between them as they peppered him with questions. They had wanted to keep him unfocused and off his guard, so when they fired the question about the shooting at him, he was unprepared and his face would betray the truth before his brain had a chance to come up with a lie.

Now, Warren looked confused. "The shot?"

"Two days ago, at Sunkissed Jewels," he replied.

"We never hit that place," Warren said.

It was the confirmation he'd wanted, but he needed to be sure. "You, your brother, and your cousin have been robbing jewelry stores. The Sunkissed Jewels was robbed. Why should we believe it wasn't you?"

"Because we never did it." Warren frowned irritably.

"You shot someone," Chloe said.

"I ain't shot nobody, ever," Warren protested.

"You're saying someone else robbed that store?" Chloe asked.

Warren shrugged. "I ain't got a clue. Alls I know is we didn't do nothing there. And we didn't shoot nobody, either."

Tom looked to his partner for confirmation she believed Warren was telling the truth. Chloe gave him a small nod. "If it wasn't you, could it have been just your brother and cousin who robbed the store without telling you?" He didn't think it was likely, but they were looking for only two people.

"No."

"How can you be sure?" Chloe asked. "Maybe they didn't want to share things three ways. Maybe they decided for that one they'd leave you out."

"They wouldn't. It was all my idea. Zane didn't even wanna do it. And Kurt, all he cared about was getting high. Anyways, we couldn't have done it. Two days ago, we was at our grandmother's funeral," Warren told them.

"In the evening?" Tom asked.

"Got home about eleven and went to bed."

Tom believed him. Zane Maloney didn't have a police record and there was no evidence he had ever been violent. The cousin, Kurt, had some drug-related misdemeanors, but again, nothing violent. He didn't even think that Warren would have shot anyone. "Did anyone else know about what you were doing?"

"No."

"No fourth person who was supposed to work with you but dropped out?"

"No."

"Was the Sunkissed Jewels on your hit list?" Chloe asked.

"Didn't really have a hit list."

"Do you know of anyone else who might also be robbing jewelry stores?"

"No."

Warren didn't have anything useful to give them, but he'd already given them the one thing they needed. Now they had proof that these kids didn't rob Hannah's store, they could move on to their next interview. One which would be infinitely harder.

Hannah.

~

9:25 A.M.

Had it worked?

He wasn't sure.

Had Hannah gotten his message?

Did she know why he did it?

Did she understand?

Did she know that he would never allow anything to hurt her?

Did she know that everything he did, he did in her best interest?

So many questions, and he had no way of knowing the answers.

The cops had caught the gang of masked men who had been robbing jewelry stores, so by now, they must know that those men hadn't been the ones who robbed Hannah's store.

But did they know who did?

Did they know it was all because of him?

Did they know that he had paid someone to do it?

Did they know why?

Were they looking for him?

This was so stressful. He hadn't realized just how much work and anxiety would go into making his plan a reality. Now he lived in constant fear that someone would connect the robbery to him. But if this worked, then it would be worth it.

He did it all for Hannah.

He had wanted her for so long, but she didn't look at him that way.

She was so self-sufficient, she just went about her life, so introverted, so scared to let anyone in, so determined to do it all by herself.

But if she would just look at him, then she would see that he was here for her no matter what. That he would do *anything* for her.

So, he had come up with an idea that would make Hannah see just how much she needed someone. That even though she was the strongest woman he'd ever met, she needed to have someone in her life that she could count on who would protect her and take care of her and make everything okay.

He had known that she would need a push to get the message.

And this seemed like the perfect option.

Put her in a situation where she was scared, where her life would be in danger, and she should come running straight to him so he could help her pick up the pieces.

It all seemed so foolproof.

What could go wrong?

At the time, he'd thought nothing. But now he was having second thoughts. If he was found out, he could go to prison. And Hannah was so tough. What if he hadn't given her enough of a push? What if she didn't come running to him? What if she tried to deal with all of it on her own?

So far, she hadn't come to him.

Did that mean he should push harder?

If the cops knew that Hannah was the target of the robbery and not the jewelry, then they would go through her life with a fine-tooth comb. They would circle around her, providing a protective shield that would be difficult for him to penetrate.

But he had to find a way to make it work.

He had to have Hannah for his very own.

He loved everything about her. She was so beautiful. He adored her long, dark auburn hair; the color reminded him of fall leaves. He loved her eyes, a gorgeous mix of green and blue and gray. He could stare into them forever. It was like staring into the bottomless depths of the ocean. He loved her milky white skin, and the light smattering of freckles across her nose. Stress and hard work made her a little too thin, but once she had him to take care of her, she would be able to relax.

Although her strength was an obstacle to getting to her, he admired it. Greatly. He knew what she had overcome, and it made him love her all the more. She was smart, and when she let her guard down and allowed herself to have a little fun, she had a marvelous sense of humor. She had a big heart and was always looking for opportunities to help others. She volunteered at a rape crisis center, she worked at a homeless shelter dishing out meals once a week, and she donated a percentage of her store's monthly profits to help underprivileged children.

He wanted her so badly, it consumed him. He ached with the desire to hold her in his arms, to kiss her, to make love to her, to be the center of her world.

He needed a way to find out if Hannah had gotten the message.

If she was scared enough that she sought solace with him.

And if she hadn't, he would take things up a level.

He was going to do whatever it took to have her.

He wouldn't stop until she was his.

~

9:36 A.M.

Tom was nervous as he stood at the door to the interview room where Hannah was waiting for them. When they'd first met, he'd never been nervous around her. Their relationship had seemed natural from the very beginning.

They'd met back in their first days of college. He'd been studying criminal justice, she'd been studying business management, and early one morning they had literally bumped into each other at the library.

The attraction had been instantaneous.

Maybe not love at first sight, but there was definitely a spark.

He'd asked her out that day, and Hannah had said yes. Their first date had been that night. And that was when he knew. He'd taken her to an amusement park and they'd stayed until closing, eating junk and riding the roller coaster over and over again. They'd had such a great time laughing and talking that he'd known that she was the woman he wanted to spend his life with.

Although, like any other couple, they had had their ups and downs, they always found a way to work through any issue that arose and remain together. He proposed a year after they met, at the library, right where they had bumped into each other. They'd married shortly after they graduated.

Everything had been going so well. He was happy in his job as an FBI agent. Hannah's store was growing, they had talked about the possibility of starting a family, and their future had seemed so bright. And then that night had changed everything.

After that, he *had* started to feel nervous around Hannah. She'd been raped and traumatized. She'd had nightmares and jumped at every little noise. He'd wanted to take away her fears, but at the same time, he hadn't known how to handle her. He had worried about failing her, about not saying or doing the right thing, about not giving her what she needed. Not because he thought she was weak but because he didn't know what his place was anymore. He was Hannah's husband, and he wanted to be there to comfort and support her, but at every opportunity, she pushed him away. That left him feeling helpless, and as such, anxious around her because he didn't want to overstep his bounds.

Nine years of closeness had been wiped away in the three years since they'd divorced, and he was feeling even more unsure around her. More so than ever since they'd spoken yesterday, and she had accused him of throwing away their marriage because he was too stubborn to admit he had needed help.

As much as he didn't want to admit it, he thought Hannah might be right.

He had made her his priority back then because she had been the one who'd been so violently assaulted. But he had been there, too. Maybe she hadn't been the only one who had needed time and help to deal with the trauma they'd been through.

Tom wasn't sure, and right now, he didn't have time to contemplate it.

"Can we hurry up and get this over with?" Hannah asked as soon as they opened the door. She looked nervous and edgy and didn't appear to be doing anything to hide it. She was wearing jeans, black, knee-high boots, and a pink sweater with sleeves that came right down over her hands—and was twisting them between her fingers as she paced the small room. He knew Hannah hated police stations after all the hours she'd spent in them recounting the story of her assault so many times.

"We'll be as quick as we can," he assured her, resisting the urge to take her elbow and guide her to the table. Instead, he went and sat. Chloe followed him, and after eyeing the door longingly, Hannah came and joined them.

"You found them, right? The men who robbed my store, who shot Jeff?"

Her hopeful, blue-green eyes cut him deeply. He was about to shatter that hope. "We found the men who robbed the other four stores," he told her gently. "We arrested them yesterday afternoon attempting to rob another. We just finished interviewing one of them. They weren't the ones who held up your store, Hannah."

Disappointment filled her face. "Are you sure?"

"We're sure, Ms. Buffy," Chloe replied.

"Then, who robbed my store?" Her eyes searched their faces seeking answers.

"We don't know."

"So, you were right." Hannah turned to him. "What happened at my store wasn't related to the others."

"I didn't want to be right, Hannah," he told her.

She arched a brow at that. "How are you going to find them?"

"Through you. Through everything you can tell us," he replied.

"We need a list of everything that was taken so we can try to track it," Chloe said.

"I started making a list, but the store was a mess. It might take me a while to get you a complete list."

"That's fine," he assured her. "I asked you before if you thought anyone might want to target you through your store and you said no. Now I need you to really think about it."

"This could still just be a random robbery, right?" Hannah asked.

"Yes," Chloe answered quickly. "It absolutely could. It probably is. But we want to be sure that it isn't anything else."

"Is there anyone who might want to hurt you?" Tom asked.

"No. I told you that already. I don't know what you want from me. There's no one who would want to hurt me. I'm sure this was just random. It's Christmas. They probably wanted to make some quick money and thought my store was an easy mark. That's it. Nothing more," Hannah finished emphatically.

She was growing agitated. And the more agitated she got, the less likely they were to get any answers from her. "Tell us about the store," he asked, redirecting her attention away from the robbery. "It's not the one you had when we were together."

"I needed a fresh start after we broke up. I met an elderly gentleman who owned a jewelry store. He was sick. Dying. He didn't have any children, but he wanted his business to continue after he died. He wanted to give it to me, but I couldn't just take it, so I sold my store and bought his. We worked together for almost a year before he passed away. That was two years ago. After he died, I renamed the store Sunkissed Jewels."

That she had chosen that particular name for her new store hadn't escaped him. He also didn't know what to make of it. Sunkissed was a nickname he'd had for her when they were together. Why had she chosen that particular name? Did that mean something? Tom wanted to ask her, but he was almost afraid to know the answer. This was just a job, and when it was over and he knew for sure that Hannah was safe, he intended to move on.

Seeing as it had been two years since she made the store her own, it was unlikely that anyone would rob the store intending to target the man she'd bought it from. "What about people in your life? Friends, neighbors, colleagues, a boyfriend?" He had to force himself to get the word out. Although they were divorced, and he didn't intend to change that, he still didn't like the idea of Hannah dating.

"I don't have a lot of friends. Most of the friends from before I kind of let go."

She didn't have to specify what the *before* was that she was talking about. Both of them had lost a lot of friends following Hannah's assault. It wasn't on purpose. It was just that both of them had withdrawn a lot from the world around them. And that meant a lot of friendships just sort of faded away until there was nothing left.

"You told us that your employee, Vincent, was the son of a friend. Which friend?" he asked.

"My next-door neighbor. Her husband died several months back. I had a young woman working with me up until about a month ago, then she moved to Australia with her fiancé. It was Christmas, and I really needed someone quickly. We were talking one evening, and she said her son needed a job for the holiday season. So, I hired Vincent on a temporary basis until I can interview for a new employee in the new year. Ellen Zimmerman and I are friends, but we're not that close. She has no reason to want revenge on me for anything, and she got a big payout from her husband's life insurance policy, so she doesn't need the money."

"Can we have the name of the woman who used to work for you?" Chloe asked.

Hannah frowned, but replied, "Amelia Topping."

"What about other friends?" he prompted. He wanted her to tell him something that convinced him this was nothing more than a random robbery.

"I don't have a lot. Work pretty much consumes my life. When I'm not there, I might have a quiet night in with a couple of old friends who are still around, but that's about it. And you know all those people, Tom. None of them would want to hurt me. I *really* don't think this has anything to do with me. I don't know anyone who would want to target me or hurt me in any way."

He really hoped that was true.

"What about a boyfriend?" Chloe asked.

"Don't have one."

Catching how uncomfortable Hannah looked, Chloe pressed her. "What about an ex?"

"There's only one since Tom," she replied reluctantly.

"What's his name?" he asked tightly. His entire body stiffened at the knowledge that Hannah had been dating since they split up. It was ridiculous; he knew that. He had dated, too, over the last three years. But right or wrong, the thought of Hannah sharing another man's bed had him seething with jealousy.

Just a job, he reminded himself.

Just. A. Job.

When this was over, they could both go their separate ways again.

"Garry Smith."

"Would he hurt you?" he demanded, aware he sounded fiercely possessive.

"I don't think so."

"You don't *think* so?" It came out as a growl.

Hannah rolled her eyes at him. "It's none of your business who I have and haven't dated since we got divorced. Don't go acting like a possessive jerk. I don't see why Garry would want to hurt me."

"Who ended the relationship. You or him?" Chloe asked.

"I did."

Knowing that Hannah had been the one to end things made him feel marginally better.

"Why?" Chloe asked.

"It wasn't going anywhere, and it didn't seem fair to lead him on. I don't want to get married again. I liked Garry, but I didn't love him. He was starting to get too clingy, too serious. He thought there was a future for us, but there wasn't. So, I told him it was over. He took it fine. He didn't seem angry or anything, just disappointed."

Despite what Hannah thought, Garry was firmly on their list of people to check out. Just because she thought he had taken the breakup well didn't mean that he had.

"Look, I don't know what else to tell you. There truly isn't anyone who's interested enough in me to rob my store. Look into Garry, if you want. Investigate all my friends. You're not going to find anything. It was just a robbery. I understand, Tom, why you think it might be more, given our history. But maybe instead of inventing reasons to keep me as the victim, you could just get yourself some help so you can move on. Can I go now?" She addressed the question to Chloe, who nodded. "I'll have the list of everything that was taken to you as soon as I can."

With that, Hannah stood and breezed out of the room.

Leaving him staring after her.

Although Hannah was a victim, he had *never* thought of her as one. She was too strong, too determined to get over what had happened to her.

He couldn't leave things like that.

Standing, he hurried after her.

~

10:10 A.M.

She was all but running through the police station, desperate to get out.

It felt like she was suffocating in here.

Hannah didn't even notice Tom until he was beside her, grabbing her arm and stopping her near frantic efforts to get back outside.

She would be happy if she never had to step foot inside a police station again in her life. She had spent so many hours in them three years ago, telling her story over and over again until the whole thing started to feel surreal, like nothing more than simply a story.

Of the six men who had assaulted her, three of them had been killed by the cops, another left in critical condition, and the other two had surrendered quietly. She had been grilled in minute detail about every aspect of the attack as they tried to ascertain whether the shootings had been justified.

They had.

The men had refused to comply with orders from the first officers on the scene to lower their weapons and surrender. Instead, they had threatened to shoot her, Tom, and the cops. The police had had no choice but to shoot them. And she was glad they did. She wished that all six men had been killed.

It would have been so much easier if they were all dead.

She hated knowing those men could get out of prison one day.

Hannah was surprised when a blast of cold air hit her face. While her mind had been stuck in the past, Tom had maneuvered her through the winding halls of the police precinct and outside. For once, she appreciated that he knew her well enough to know what she needed without her having to verbalize it.

She dragged in a deep breath, filling her lungs with the icy winter air and letting the wide open outdoors soothe her.

"Are you okay?" Tom's light brown eyes were examining her closely.

"Yes," she replied shortly, snatching her arm back and turning, intending to leave.

"Hannah, wait." He grabbed her arm again, holding her in place.

She didn't want to deal with this now. She just wanted to get back to her store, get the list of missing items to her insurance company and the FBI, then get back to her life. "What do you want, Tom?"

"I'm not trying to make you a victim. I never did." His face was so earnest.

Maybe he really didn't realize what he'd done. Maybe he'd been so caught up in his own pain that he hadn't even realized what he was doing. Hannah had always known that he was suffering just as much as she was, but maybe Tom hadn't. He didn't want to admit that he was struggling. He was an FBI agent; he was supposed to be strong and tough. But his desire to convey an air of strong and tough and treat her as a helpless victim who needed him to do everything for her had done more harm than good.

"How can we have lived the same events and yet we both have two completely different takes of what happened?" Tom looked sad now.

"Because you didn't want to see things from my point of view. You had already made up your mind. I was the victim, and it was your job to save me. It didn't matter what I wanted."

"That's not true."

"Of course, it was. It was true then, and it's true now. You still want me to be the victim. You can't accept that this was just a robbery. Nothing more. No conspiracy. No hidden motives. No boogeyman hiding in the corner. Just a robbery."

"Do you always have to be so stubborn?" he growled.

"I'm not being stubborn. Just realistic. You're the one who's seeing things that aren't there."

"Do you trust me?"

The question caught her by surprise, but she didn't hesitate to answer. "Yes."

"Then trust me now. All I'm asking is that you be careful. Is that really too much?"

Hannah sighed. No matter what she said or did, Tom could never let go of the notion that she was a victim. "Why are you doing this? We've been divorced for three years, we've both moved on with our lives. It's over between us, why can't you just let it go?"

"I'm doing my job. Nothing more and nothing less."

"I'm not your responsibility anymore," she reminded him.

"This is my case, so you most certainly are my responsibility."

"No. You were working a string of armed robberies at jewelry stores. You closed that case. The robbery at my store wasn't related. That means the local police department can handle the case, and you and your partner can go back to the FBI."

"I'm not walking away until this case is closed, and I'm convinced that you're safe."

"Why do you care?" If Tom had really cared about her, he would never have walked away from her in the first place.

"How can you ask me that?" He looked hurt.

"You don't have to worry about me. I know you see me as a victim, but this time I'm not. I wasn't hurt. There is no one after me. I am not in danger. Nothing is going to happen to me." How many times was she going to have to tell him that before he got it through his thick head?

"You said you trusted me. Can't you for once just listen to me, let me help you? Why is that so hard for you to do? Why is it such a repulsive idea to you to let me help you?"

"You don't want to help me; you want to save me. I get it. You feel like what happened was your fault. But it wasn't. I never blamed you, Tom. Ever. How could you have predicted what would happen? You couldn't. I never once thought it was your fault. That was your issue. And you wouldn't acknowledge it and get help. I'm not the one who's stubborn; you are."

Tom shook his head. "You're the stubborn one. I wanted to help you, and you acted like that was the worst thing ever."

"I wanted to learn to be strong again. I have felt like a victim every day since it happened. And the more you treated me like a victim, the more I felt like one. You didn't want to be my husband anymore. You just wanted to take care of me. But we should have been taking care of each other. We could have been a team, helping each other, but you couldn't accept that you were a victim, too."

"No, I wasn't." He looked horrified by the very suggestion.

"Yes, you were."

"No."

"Yes."

"No."

"Yes." In the nine years they'd been together, they had never argued much, but ever since the home invasion, they had developed a tendency to argue constantly, like a couple of preschoolers. "They tied you to a chair, Tom, beat you, and made you watch them rape me. Whether you want to admit it or not, you were just as much a victim as I was. You could have gotten help. We could have helped each other. You could have looked at me as a survivor. Instead, you chose to make me the victim and make it your project to fix me. When that didn't work, you just left. That was your choice. I never said I wanted you to go. Wanting to do things for myself wasn't an invitation for you to leave, but you did. You just left me."

"You never asked me to stay," he said quietly.

He was right.

She had never asked him to stay.

She had wanted to, but she'd been too hurt that he left, and then she had been too determined to prove that she didn't need anyone. That she could be completely self-sufficient. That she could take the horror that she had suffered and use it to make herself stronger than she had been before. She had needed to know—for herself, not for anyone else—that she could survive.

And she had.

But that didn't change the fact that she still loved Tom, and if he hadn't walked out the door, they would probably still be together today.

"If I had, would you have stayed?" she asked.

Hannah looked at the man who would always hold a big piece of her heart. His hands were on his hips. She remembered what it was like to feel those calloused fingertips tracing over her bare skin. His lips were pulled into a tight line, and as she looked at them, all she could think of was the spark of electricity she always felt when they pressed against hers. She had never felt safer than she had when she had been wrapped up in Tom's arms. It had been like having steel bands around her; yet, at the same time, they were warm and comforting.

She should have asked him to stay. Begged him. Done whatever it took to convince him that her desire to be self-sufficient and do things for herself had nothing to do with him. It was all about not losing herself and becoming just another rape victim.

Maybe letting him walk out of her life had been the biggest mistake she'd ever made. She had survived. She had grown strong. She had thrived in her business life. But she wasn't really happy. There was a big gaping hole in her heart and her life that she wasn't sure she could ever fill.

Tears were building in her eyes, but when she looked at Tom's, she found them all cop. He hadn't answered her question, but she supposed that *was* her answer. Tom had left because he wanted to. Even if she had been able to swallow her pride and ask him to stay, he wouldn't have.

Straightening her spine, she made her voice calm, cool, and collected. "There are no monsters after me, Tom. So you can go back to your life with a clear conscience."

"I'm going to do my job, Hannah."

"You always do. Just don't make it any more than that."

"Don't worry, I won't. This is just another job."

Just another job.

Well, at least she knew where she stood.

Maybe she had needed to hear him say it. To know that he was happy with his decision to end their marriage. To know he had no regrets. Maybe now she could finally properly move on with her life.

With a last look at Tom, Hannah turned and walked away.

10:38 A.M.

Would he have stayed if Hannah had asked him to?

Tom still couldn't believe she had asked him that.

And he couldn't believe that he hadn't given her an answer.

What was wrong with him?

Would he have stayed if she had asked him to?

Yes.

Of course.

He had only left in the first place because it was what he thought she wanted. He had thought that she didn't want him around. That she wanted, or even needed, to deal with what had happened on her own. That time and space and isolation to process it all were what was going to help her recover.

So, he had given it to her.

Only now, he wasn't so sure it *was* what she had wanted.

When she'd asked him if he would have stayed with her if she had asked him to, it had looked like she hoped he would say yes.

Why hadn't he?

"Tom." Chloe appeared behind him.

Hannah had walked away, and he'd let her. He had to accept that it was over between them. Whether or not it would have changed things, if she'd asked him to stay was irrelevant now. She hadn't, and he'd left. They were divorced. This was just a job. When it was finished, he would leave again.

Just a job.

Just a job.

Just a job.

Maybe if he kept saying that, it might make it true.

Because he knew it was no longer just a job. He wanted to keep Hannah safe because he still loved her. He wanted any excuse to keep seeing her again. And when this case was closed, he didn't want to walk away.

This *wasn't* just a job.

"Are you coming in?" Chloe asked.

He wanted to say no.

He wanted to go after Hannah.

He wanted to find a way to fix things with her.

But he didn't.

"Yeah." He was a coward, so he may as well let Hannah go—again —and go and work on this case. At least he could find who had robbed Hannah's store and make sure that no one ever hurt her again.

With his heart still pulling him in the opposite direction, he followed his partner back inside. At his desk, he attempted to not let himself get distracted by his complicated relationship with Hannah. That wasn't going to help her right now.

"I checked out Hannah's old employee, Amelia Topping, while you were talking with Hannah," Chloe told him. "I don't think there's any reason for her to be involved in the robbery. She hasn't left Australia in the five weeks since she moved there. She's busy planning her wedding and has already bought her own jewelry store in her new town. When I spoke to her, she was upset to hear about what had happened and concerned about Hannah and Jeff. I don't think she's involved."

"We should look into the neighbor," he said.

"Ellen Zimmerman. Hannah said they were friends but not that close. She also said that the woman received a sizeable life insurance payout when her husband died. I looked into her, and she also owns several rental properties, plus she sold her husband's chain of shoe stores for a lot of money."

"I agree, it doesn't seem likely, but she was the one who suggested that her son go to work at Hannah's store, and then a month later, the store is robbed. We can't discount it."

"Might not be about money," Chloe suggested. "Maybe Hannah and her husband had an affair, and it's personal. She and the son decide to teach her a lesson and set up the robbery."

Tom glared at Chloe, furious at the very suggestion Hannah would have an affair. "She wouldn't do that."

"Maybe it wasn't the husband. Maybe Hannah and the son were involved. And Ellen didn't like that, decided to teach Hannah a lesson."

"She didn't mention dating nineteen-year-old Vincent," he said tightly.

"No, she didn't. But she clearly wasn't comfortable being forthcoming about her love life with you in the room. Maybe I should talk to her again. Without you. See if she mentions anything else."

"I don't think she was lying when she said that she hadn't dated much. Or too uncomfortable to say it in front of me." He knew

Hannah, and he knew what she'd been through. He'd had a front row seat. It made sense that after being gang raped by six men, she wasn't in a hurry to start dating again.

"It does make sense given her history," Chloe agreed. "And she has clearly put a lot of time and effort into building up her business, but we have to look into everything. Maybe she's been dating a lot but just doesn't want to hurt your feelings by telling you."

"Why would hurting my feelings be an issue? We're divorced. She's free to date whoever she wants."

Chloe rolled her eyes. "The tone of your voice and the look on your face when you say she's free to date whoever she wants, make your feelings on her love life pretty clear."

Tom said nothing. He had nothing to say to that. He *hated* the idea of Hannah with another man. "We have to talk to her ex." He couldn't deny that part of him was insanely curious about who Hannah had dated after their divorce, while at the same time, part of him didn't want to meet the man and acknowledge he was real and Hannah really had had a life after him.

"We'll call Garry Smith and set up a meeting. Even though Hannah said the break up went smoothly, it doesn't mean it did on Garry's part. Maybe he doesn't want to let her go. Maybe he thinks, if he can scare her badly enough, she'll come running back to him. If nothing else, he might be able to give us some insight into anyone who might have a grudge against Hannah. I know she says there's no one, but I think part of it is she doesn't want to admit you could be right, so she might be missing something."

It was a possibility, but Tom didn't think Hannah would take any risks with her own safety, even to prove him wrong. And the assault had made her vigilant. She would have noticed anyone acting suspiciously around her. If someone was targeting Hannah, then they were doing their best to remain inconspicuous. "There's something bothering me about the robbery."

"What?"

"They break in after hours. They know that most jewelry stores will have a silent alarm. They tried to get the codes to the safe, but on the way in, they smashed the glass cases and grabbed some stuff. Why bother? If what you wanted was the expensive stuff in the safe, then why waste the limited time you have to grab some of the small-time stuff?"

"Maybe they thought there was a chance they wouldn't get the code in time."

"Why would they think that? If Hannah didn't have a phobia of guns, she would have given them the code. So why bother with the cheap stuff? It's almost like they wanted to make it look like a robbery, to look like the others."

"Or they just wanted to get away with as much as they could," Chloe countered.

"I guess." His partner was being so logical. He didn't want to be logical right now. Even the possibility that Hannah could be in danger, left him so far out from logical he couldn't even make contact with it right now.

"Hey, guys."

Savannah Watson, a friend of Chloe's who worked for the FBI's Evidence Response Team Unit, was walking toward them. Savannah was a pretty blonde, with large blue eyes, who walked with a cane following a violent assault that had shattered her hip and ruined her dreams of becoming an FBI agent. She had, instead, transferred to the forensic unit.

"I brought gingerbread." Savannah set a box down on Chloe's desk. "And I have news for you two." She dropped into his chair when he stood and indicated she should sit.

"You found something at Hannah's store?" he asked hopefully, anxious for a direction to move in.

"Yes. I went back and re-swept her store since we know that the robbery there wasn't related to the others, and since there was some question over whether or not she was the real target."

"Tom is the only one who thinks that," Chloe inserted.

"I think he's right," Savannah said.

"What did you find?" His heart clenched. Up until Savannah said that, he hadn't been sure if he really was just being wildly unobjective where his ex was concerned or if his gut feeling was right.

"An FM short-range listening device."

"Someone bugged her store?" Tom couldn't quite believe what he was hearing.

"Yes. And recently. The battery life is about one hundred and twenty hours; it was ninety percent flat. The robbery was two days ago. That means it was put there not more than three days before," Savannah explained.

"So, the robbers were in her store at some point in those couple of days before the robbery," Chloe stated.

"Or whoever they were working with. Where was the listening device found?" he asked.

"Under Hannah's desk. It's a short-range device, so the robbers would have had to be close by to hear what was happening in there."

"Which means they knew she was in there. If they'd just wanted to rob the store, they could have waited until it was empty. Instead, they made sure that she was going to be there."

He'd been right.

This wasn't a random robbery.

Someone had deliberately decided to target Hannah and her store.

But why?

And who?

And how was he going to find out?

~

2:29 P.M.

Hannah was nervous.

She wanted to see Jeff, but she didn't.

She hadn't spoken to him since the shooting, but she had been calling the hospital to ask for regular updates on how he was doing.

At least this was a good distraction from thinking about Tom. She wished she could forget about him. For good.

No, she corrected herself.

That wasn't true.

Even if she could wipe all traces of Tom from her past and her mind, she wouldn't. She couldn't. Before the home invasion, they had had a lot of good times together. They had been happy together. They would have spent the rest of their lives together.

But that night had changed everything.

She meant what she had said to Tom earlier. What had happened wasn't his fault, despite what he thought.

There was no way that he could have known what was going to happen. It had been one in the morning, and they'd woken to a sound outside. It had sounded like a crying dog. Tom had gone down to check it out, wondering if the puppy next door had gotten out of its yard.

It hadn't.

When he opened their backdoor, he'd been ambushed by six armed men who had knocked him unconscious.

She had remained in bed and expected her husband to return, possibly with the puppy in tow. Instead, six men with guns had dragged her unconscious husband into their bedroom.

What transpired over the next several hours she had tried her best to block from her mind. *That* she really did wish she could forget about.

But as much as she wanted to, she couldn't.

It was there forever.

And it had cost her the one person she loved the most in the world.

The assault had gotten between her and Tom and grown and festered until it was too big for them to overcome. It had torn them apart instead of bringing them together. They had both been struggling to deal with their own feelings and emotions, let alone each other's. Tom might have been the one who walked away, but the blame for their breakup could be placed equally on both their shoulders.

Now he was back in her life; at least, for the time being. But nothing seemed different. They still argued whenever they were together. They still couldn't sit down and sort out their issues. There was still a huge gap between them that she didn't think could ever be bridged.

One thing she did know was that Tom would find the men who had robbed her store, who had held a gun to her head, who had shot her employee and friend.

Absently, Hannah touched her hand to her temple. The bruise had darkened over the last two days and was now a vivid mottled mix of black and blue and purple. It was tender to touch, and she still had a slight headache, but it was nothing compared to what Jeff had gone through.

At least he was going to be okay.

She had to keep reminding herself of that.

Like a mantra.

Jeff was okay. Jeff was okay. Jeff was okay.

She'd been reminding herself of that for the last forty-eight hours, trying to get it to sink in, but all she could do was feel guilt.

What if he blamed her?

She blamed herself, so she couldn't hold it against him if he blamed her, too.

He *should* blame her.

It *was* her fault, after all.

She would work on her gun phobia. She owed that to Jeff at the very least. And she would do whatever else she could to try to make it up to him. Of course, she would pay him his full wage for however long he needed to take off to recover. Or, if he wanted to resign, she would pay him out to make sure he had plenty of money to last until he found another job. She would do anything she could to help him.

Hannah wasn't quite sure what to expect when she walked into his hospital room. She knew he'd been shot in the upper chest, near his right shoulder, and she knew that the doctors said he would make a full recovery. But was he awake, or did they have him sedated? Was he hooked up to machines, or had he progressed to the stage where he was stable and able to move about freely? Was he confined to the bed?

She couldn't hover here in the corridor forever. She may as well get it over with. If he yelled at her, he yelled at her. She would stand there and take what she deserved.

Before she could talk herself out of it, Hannah opened the door to Jeff's room and stepped inside, where she relaxed marginally. The bed was empty. Jeff was sitting in a chair by the window, a book perched awkwardly in his left hand. His right arm was in a sling to help protect his injured shoulder.

He looked all right.

Hannah sighed in relief.

As the door swung closed, Jeff turned in her direction. She expected to see anger in his brown eyes, but instead they were full of concern.

"Hannah!" He set the book down and stood, swaying only slightly, then hurried to her side. "Are you okay?"

For a moment, she was too choked up to speak. How could he be concerned about her when he was the one who had almost been killed? "I'm fine. How are you?"

"Be good as new in a couple of days," he assured her. Jeff gave her a wide smile, his brown eyes twinkling just as brightly as they always did. His silvery brown hair was a tangled mess around his head, making him look more relaxed and casual than she was used to seeing him; but in the end, he looked like the Jeff she knew.

Searching his eyes to see if he was just placating her, she didn't see anything untoward and relaxed further. "I'm so sorry, Jeff."

His eyes crinkled. "Sorry about what?"

"They shot you because I didn't give them the code. I wanted to, but I couldn't talk. You came in to save me but they shot you instead. I'm so sorry." She couldn't stop a few tears from tumbling out and trickling slowly down her cheeks.

"They shot me because they chose to. That had nothing to do with you," Jeff said firmly.

"But if I had just—"

"No," Jeff cut her off. "I don't want to hear any more about you blaming yourself. It was not your fault, Hannah. It was not your fault."

She didn't believe that, but she didn't argue. "You should be sitting down. Are you really okay?"

"Doctors say I was lucky; the bullet didn't hit anything vital. I lost a bit of blood, but rest and some physical therapy and I'll be fine in a few weeks," he told her as they went and sat in the two chairs by the window. "Some FBI agents came by. Agents Drake and Luckman. They said our robbery wasn't related to the others."

"I know." She still couldn't believe that this was about her. Who would want to hurt her? The list was short. *Very* short. There was no one. Not a single person. Maybe someone hadn't known that she had taken over Reginald Thames' store and they'd really been after him. Jeff had worked for Mr. Thames then stayed on when she took over. Maybe he knew something. "Could there be anyone who would want to hurt Mr. Thames?"

"No," Jeff replied immediately. "You knew him. He was a sweet old man. He wouldn't hurt a fly. There's no one who would have any reason to want to hurt him."

He was right. Hannah knew that. "What about you? Is there anyone who might want to hurt you?"

"The agents asked me the same thing, but I told them there wasn't anyone who would have any reason to rob your store just to hurt me. And even if there was someone with a grudge against me, why would they target your store to get to me?"

"I don't know," she answered helplessly. None of this made sense.

"What about Vincent?"

"Vincent?"

"We don't really know much about him. You never checked references or work history or anything with him." Jeff's tone was slightly reprimanding.

"He's Ellen's son." She hadn't seen a reason to look into Vincent's references. He was the son of her neighbor and friend, and she had only intended for him to work for the month or two over Christmas and into the new year and then she would look for a permanent replacement for Amelia. "Do you think it could be Vincent they were really after?"

"No."

She was surprised by the confidence in Jeff's tone—maybe he knew the teenager better than she'd thought.

"I don't think this was personal. We know it wasn't related to the other robberies, but that doesn't mean they were targeting any of us. I think it was random. I don't think you need to worry about anyone coming after you or me or Vincent. It was just random, Hannah, I'm sure of it."

Hannah hoped Jeff was right.

She *really* did.

She'd dealt with enough crime in the last few years; she didn't want to have to deal with anything else.

～

9:18 P.M.

This was probably a stupid idea.

And she wasn't going to be pleased if she found out.

Yet Tom had no plans on leaving.

Hannah was never going to know he was here. And given that someone had bugged her office, he couldn't stand the thought of her being home alone and unprotected in the event that whoever planted the listening device came after her here.

Was that likely?

Probably not.

But why take the chance?

He would much rather park his car across the street from Hannah's house and sleep in it. Then, if anything happened, he'd be right here. He had failed Hannah once already. He wasn't going to do it again.

If only he had done things differently that night, then those men would never have gotten inside the house. A noise in the backyard in the middle of the night should have been more than enough warning that something was wrong. He should have taken his gun with him just to be safe.

But he hadn't.

And Hannah had paid the price.

Those hours, sitting there, tied to the chair, watching those men rape his wife repeatedly and so roughly she'd been left badly bleeding while he was powerless to do anything about it, were the worst of his life.

They were pure hell.

He hadn't expected to walk out of their bedroom alive.

By some miracle, they had survived.

Then the hard work of recovering had begun.

He and Hannah had both struggled, and those struggles had ended up tearing them apart. When his wife needed him the most, he had bailed. He had honestly believed it was because it was what she wanted and what was best for her.

But now, he wasn't so sure.

Hannah had called her store the nickname he'd given her, and today she'd asked him if he would have stayed if she'd asked. She was sending him all these mixed signals. Now he didn't know what to think.

The one thing Tom knew was that under no circumstances would he allow anyone to hurt Hannah ever again.

CHAPTER
Four

December 21st
8:44 A.M.

His back was aching today. Sleeping in his car, while Tom believed it to be a necessity, was still the most uncomfortable night he'd spent in years.

Hannah had always hogged the bed, plastering herself all over him: her head on his chest, her leg thrown across his, her hair tickling his nose all night. She was a cold sleeper so even on the hottest of nights she never kept to her side of the bed, instead draping herself on top of him. He, on the other hand, was a hot sleeper, and most nights her body heat had made his own rise to the point where he was sweltering.

He had loved every second of it—falling asleep with her at his side, feeling her warm body against his if he woke during the night.

It was heaven.

And never once, not even on the hottest of summer nights, had he ever rolled her body off his.

Tom knew he didn't want it to be over between them.

He wanted there to be a way for them to have a second chance.

But he wasn't sure if it was already too late.

Last night, as he'd sat in his car watching Hannah's house, he'd known that he didn't want to walk away when this was done. He hadn't slept much; his eyes had remained glued to the house, watching the light in what he assumed was Hannah's bedroom remain on till the early hours of the morning, and he realized that he wanted to be there to support her.

He never should have walked away in the first place. He knew that now. Believing it was what Hannah wanted was a cop-out. Even if he'd been right—and now, he wasn't sure that he was—that Hannah wanted to deal with what had happened on her own without him, he should have insisted on staying, on being there for her, on helping them both heal. Because he now admitted that he had needed to heal just as much as Hannah had.

Even if it wasn't possible for them to find a way to reconcile, Tom knew he had to try. And step number one was finding who bugged Hannah's office and if they were really targeting her.

"Garry Smith?" he asked as he opened the door to the interview room where the man was waiting for them.

"Yes. I was told this was about Hannah and the robbery. Is she all right?"

Tom assessed the man. Garry Smith was thirty—the same age as Hannah and himself. He had thick blond hair, bright blue eyes, and no doubt a perfect six pack under his grey sweater. He looked like he could be a male model. Despite the fact that Tom knew he was in just as good shape, he couldn't help the spear of jealousy he felt coming face-to-face with Hannah's ex-boyfriend.

There were so many things he wanted to know, and yet didn't. Had Garry and Hannah been intimate? And he didn't just mean sexually, although he wondered about that, too. But had Hannah confided in Garry? Had she shared her thoughts and feelings with him? How close had the two of them been? And were things really completely over between them?

"Hannah is fine," he answered, and he would make sure she stayed that way. "But the robbery wasn't connected to the others, and we're looking into the possibility that robbery wasn't the prime motivation for the attack on her store."

"What else could it be?" Garry's forehead crinkled in confusion.

"Do you think there's a chance anyone might want to target Hannah?" Chloe asked.

"Hannah?" Garry repeated as though the very notion was preposterous. "Why would anyone want to hurt Hannah?"

"It was her store; we have to look into that possibility," he replied, deciding he didn't like Garry Smith. He was pretty sure that had more to do with hating the idea of this man with his ex-wife than because he thought the man was involved in bugging and robbing Hannah's store.

"How long did you and Hannah date?" Chloe asked.

"A little over a year."

A little over a year? The longest he had ever dated anyone since the divorce was four months. Hannah had been with Garry for over three times that. Just how close had the two of them been? He was almost afraid to find out.

"And who ended things?" Chloe asked.

They already knew that Hannah had, but it would be interesting to see Garry's take on things to gain some insight into whether he might have reason—in his mind, at least—to cause Hannah harm.

"She did."

"Why?" Tom asked, pleased to have confirmation that it had been Hannah who had ended the relationship. He wasn't sure why that made him feel better. Maybe because it somehow meant that Hannah wasn't really over him. Which meant that maybe, somehow, there was hope for the two of them after all.

"I guess she wasn't as into the relationship as I was."

"Is that what she said?" Chloe asked.

Garry shrugged. His blue eyes had darkened a little, taken on a dismal gleam. "Pretty much. I started talking about our future, and whenever I would bring it up, Hannah would get uncomfortable and change the subject. The first few times I just let it go, thinking she needed a little more time, but when she continued to show no interest in taking our relationship to the next level, I confronted her. She finally told me that she didn't want things to get serious between us and that she was ending things."

"Did you try to change her mind?" he asked.

"I tried to talk to her about it. I tried to find out why she didn't want to keep seeing me; I didn't understand. Everything had been going so well between us. I knew that I loved Hannah, and I thought she felt the same way."

"It must have made you angry when you found out that she didn't," Chloe said.

"Angry? No. Disappointed, sad, confused, let down, yes."

"How let down?" Chloe asked.

Garry narrowed his eyes at them. "I know where you're going with that, and I know what you're thinking. But I would *never* hurt Hannah. I loved her."

"Do you still love her?" Tom asked.

He hesitated for a moment. "If I say yes, it's going to make me look bad. Like I haven't let go. Like I'm some kind of creep who might want to get revenge on her for breaking up with me, but it's not like that. If Hannah gave me another chance, would I go back to her in a second? Yes. But I'm not angry with her. She didn't want to keep seeing me. There was nothing I could do to change her mind, and I've accepted that."

Garry claimed he had accepted it, yet he had admitted that the breakup was not his idea. He hadn't wanted it to happen, and he had tried to change her mind. If Hannah would agree to date him again, then he would. It didn't sound like he was over Hannah at all. "How did you try to change her mind, Mr. Smith?"

"I didn't hurt her, if that's what you're implying. How many times do I have to say it? I would *never* hurt Hannah. Ever. For any reason. I loved her. Okay, I still love her. She's beautiful and smart and strong, and any man would be lucky to have her. I know I was."

Tom knew he had been lucky to have Hannah, too. He just wished he'd been smart enough to remember that while he still had her. "If you didn't set up this robbery to hurt Hannah, then do you have any ideas of anyone who might?"

"No, I told you everyone loved Hannah. No one would want to hurt her. She was so sweet, wouldn't hurt a fly, and she'd . . ." Garry trailed off, looking thoughtful.

"Did you think of something, Mr. Smith?" Chloe asked.

He looked up at them, earnest now. "Her therapist."

Hannah was still seeing a therapist? He shouldn't be surprised. She'd been very diligent with her therapy after the assault. He had met Dr. Langley and liked the woman a lot—thought she was great for Hannah. Tom couldn't see her doing anything to hurt Hannah now. Why would she?

"What about her therapist?" Chloe asked.

"He's creepy. I don't like him," Garry replied.

He? Hannah must have stopped seeing Dr. Langley along the way and moved on to someone new. "What's his name?"

"Bryce McCracken."

"And what about him makes him creepy?"

"His methods," Garry answered quickly. "I didn't agree with them at all."

"What were his methods?"

"He believed in this 'exposure therapy technique.' You know, where you take someone and expose them to whatever it is they're afraid of until it doesn't bother them anymore. I thought after what Hannah had been through she shouldn't be letting anyone put her through that."

Tom stiffened. Had Hannah told Garry about the home invasion? He didn't like that idea. At all. He hadn't told any of the women he'd dated. But Hannah had been with Garry for over a year, long enough for them to grow close and for Garry to start thinking that they had a future. "What had Hannah been through?"

"I don't know the details. Just that it was something bad. I tried to get her to talk to me about it, but she wouldn't. All I know is, she is petrified of guns and most nights can't sleep in a bed."

Finding out Hannah still struggled to sleep in a bed was overshadowed by the fact that Garry knew that. If he knew that, then he must have spent the night at Hannah's. Tom struggled to control his breathing as images of Hannah and Garry being intimate filled his head.

He had to let go of the jealousy.

He knew that.

But he couldn't.

Nor could he stand to be in the same room as Hannah's ex-boyfriend for a moment longer.

"We need contact information for Bryce McCracken," he said. Or snarled.

"Yeah, sure." Garry Smith looked confused by his sudden hostility. Which somehow only made him hate the man more.

Tom stood, threw back his chair, and stalked out of the room.

His feet knew where they were going even before his mind consciously processed it.

He had to see Hannah.

Now.

~

9:51 A.M.

She was wandering aimlessly around her store. Although Hannah had been hoping to get it back up and running to make the most of the last few days before Christmas, she had to face the reality that it wasn't going to happen.

Too much needed to be done before she could reopen. The glass display cases needed to be rebuilt, and she couldn't get anyone to come and do it until January. She still had to finish making a list of everything that had been taken. She was down one employee. And to be honest, she just didn't have the energy to face customers and long work days right now.

But she also couldn't just spend her days hanging around her house.

So, she was here, pacing up and down her store and procrastinating the tedious and time-consuming task of figuring out what was missing.

Part of her wanted to just give up. Declare it too much to handle and shove it into the "too-hard basket," sell the store, cut her losses, and find something else to do with her life. But the other part of her knew that wasn't an option. She couldn't allow it to be an option. If she gave up, it would make the last three years one big pointless waste of her time.

She couldn't allow that. She had fought too long and too hard to get where she was to throw it all away. As tempting as it was some days to just throw in the towel, curl up under the covers in her armchair and never get up again, Hannah knew she wouldn't do it. She would never give up. Not even if she had to struggle through every single day of the rest of her life.

Some days she wished there was something that made it all worthwhile.

Her job was important to her, and she loved it. She loved seeing her store grow, and she loved making jewelry that brought people joy and made their special occasions extra special, but she wanted something just for her. Something that made her eager to get up in the morning, that made her heart light, that made her forget about the horror of the past and be excited about the future.

For a while, she'd thought it might be Garry Smith. He was sweet and funny and kind, and she had enjoyed spending time with him. But instead of the more time she spent with him making her like him more and start to fall in love with him, it had the opposite effect. The more time they spent together, the more she knew that nothing was ever going to happen between them. She didn't feel anything. Hannah knew she should have told him sooner, that it hadn't been fair to let him think that they had a future when she knew they didn't, but she just hadn't had the heart to tell him.

She had worked so diligently on overcoming the assault that it seemed only fair that she get something that made her truly happy. Something that made her life full. Something—or some*one*—that made her live again.

The door opened, and as she turned, she knew who she was going to see standing there.

Tom.

She didn't like the way her heart stuttered every time they were in the same room. He had made it perfectly clear that he was here *only* because it was his job. That even if she had asked him to stay three years ago, he would have left anyway.

It was over.

She had to keep reminding herself of that; otherwise, she was going to get her heart broken all over again.

Tom stood still for a long moment, staring at her with an inscrutable expression on his face—so intently, she squirmed.

Then he was walking toward her.

Hannah felt like she should back away, unsure what he was going to do.

But she didn't.

She just stood there and watched him.

When he reached her, he paused for barely a moment before wrapping one arm around her waist, yanking her up against his body. His other hand curled around her neck. Then his mouth was on hers.

The kiss was hot and fiery and over before she even knew if she'd kissed him back or not.

Tom released her, and Hannah just stood there staring at him.

Had that really just happened?

If it weren't for Tom's heavy breathing, echoed by her own, she would have thought she just imagined the whole thing.

Why had he done that?

They were divorced. It had been over between them for three long years. He had been the one to walk out on her. And she had collected up the scattered pieces of her heart and her life and put them back together again. Who did Tom think he was to come back into her life, repeatedly tell her he was here only because it was his job, and then kiss her?

Angry now, she glared at him. "What are you doing here? Again."

"I came to see you."

"You can't just kiss me, Tom. We're not a couple anymore."

He ignored her and instead said, "You're still seeing a therapist."

She shrugged. What she was or wasn't doing was none of his business. He had made it *very* clear that she either did her recovery his way or he wasn't interested. Since she hadn't, he'd walked out the door. Why did he care now? What difference did it make to him if she still needed the help of a professional to deal with what had happened?

"You didn't mention that," he continued.

"Why would I?"

"Because I asked you if there was anyone who might want to hurt you."

She wasn't understanding what he was getting at. "Why would my therapist want to hurt me? I see him so he can *help* me."

"He believed in exposure therapy."

"You spoke to Garry." There was no other explanation. Garry was the only one who knew she saw a therapist and what treatment methods he used.

"Did Bryce McCracken talk to you about helping you with your phobia of guns?"

"No. Why?" She still didn't know where this was going.

"Could he have set this up? Thrown you into a situation where you'd have to be exposed to a gun so you could work on your fears? Did you know he was going to do it?"

Furious, she responded, "If this was all a setup to help me overcome my phobia, then wouldn't I have told you that? And Jeff was *shot*. If this was a game, then why would he have been hurt?"

"Maybe that wasn't part of the plan. Maybe you thought you'd just make the most of the spate of jewelry store robberies. Maybe you thought no one would get hurt. Maybe you got scared when Jeff was shot and didn't want to admit the truth."

She slapped him.

It happened before she could even register what she was doing.

Hannah had never struck another living being in her life, but no one had ever made such a repulsively ridiculous accusation toward her before.

Tears burned the backs of her eyes. How could *Tom,* of all people, suggest such a thing? He knew her. They'd been married. He'd lived through the horrific home invasion with her. He knew better than anyone how she'd suffered. To know that he thought so little of her, that she would purposely expose her employees to a traumatic experience where they would be psychologically scarred for life just to work on her own problems, was devastating.

"How could you even ask me that?" she demanded.

Tom's eyes remained cold and empty as he examined her closely, trying to gauge whether she was lying. Apparently, he decided that she wasn't because his face grew sad. "I'm sorry, Hannah. I didn't think you really did, but I had to ask. I needed to see your honest reaction. I was just doing my job. If it hadn't been me who asked, my partner was going to, and I thought it would be better if it was me."

"Well, it wasn't," she replied sullenly, feeling only marginally better to know that Tom didn't really think she would fake the robbery.

"I'm sorry."

"Tom, why did you kiss me?"

"Why did you choose the name Sunkissed Jewels for your store?"

Not going to be distracted, she asked, "Was kissing me just part of your plan, as well? Was that just you 'doing your job'?"

"No."

"Then why did you do it?"

His gaze squarely met hers. "Because I wanted to."

Talk about mixed signals. He kissed her, then accused her of setting up the robbery. Why didn't he just leave her alone? He was working the robbery, but that didn't mean he had to keep seeing her. His partner could always come if they needed some information from her. Having him constantly around made everything too confusing. Her heart wanted Tom back while her head wasn't sure it was a good idea.

"Hannah, why did you use my nickname for you as the name of your store?"

He was staring at her so intently. As though the answer she gave could change things. But change what? They were divorced. It was over. That was what Tom had wanted. She was tempted to lie to him, but she had never been dishonest with him before, and she couldn't start now. "Because it reminded me of happy times. Of the life I had before. Because it reminded me of you."

~

12:21 P.M.

He had kissed her.

Tom still couldn't believe he'd done it.

What had he been thinking?

That was not the way to win Hannah back.

Neither was accusing her of putting her employees in danger by faking the robbery as part of her therapy. He hadn't wanted to ask her. He hadn't seen the point. He already knew what the answer was, but Chloe had said if he didn't ask her about it, she would, and he had honestly thought it would be better coming from him.

Again, he'd been wrong.

It seemed he wasn't as good at reading his ex-wife as he hoped he would be.

Why had he kissed her? He was pretty sure it was a mistake and only going to grow the gap between them, not close it. She hadn't even kissed him back. He'd thought that meant she wasn't interested in seeing if they could work things out, but then she'd told him she'd used his nickname for her store because it reminded her of him, of how happy they had been, of their lives before that night.

There was hope. He knew there was. But they had to sit down and actually talk without it devolving into an argument. And he had to stop telling her it was just a job when he knew that was a bold-faced lie.

It wasn't just a job.

Hannah could never be just a job to him.

Trying to forget about her over the last three years had been a pointless waste of time. He could never forget her. He loved her. She and she alone laid claim to his heart.

Now, his sole focus had to be on solving this case. Once that was done, he and Hannah could find a way to work things out.

The door to the office opened, and both he and Chloe stood. A man of around forty, with bright orangey-red hair, striking blue eyes, and so many freckles it was almost impossible to see any space between them, looked back at them.

"You're the agents who called?" Dr. Bryce McCracken asked.

"Yes. Special Agent Drake, and this is my partner, Special Agent Luckman." Tom made the introductions, eager to get started. Just because Hannah said that her therapist didn't try to create a situation where she would be forced to confront her fears didn't mean he hadn't done it without her knowledge.

"Come in, I have about thirty minutes until my next patient arrives for their session," the doctor told them as they followed him into his office.

Bryce was fairly recently divorced, and his ex-wife bore a striking resemblance to Hannah. Tom was concerned that since he had lost his marriage that he had fixated on Hannah in an attempt to save her and then possibly pursue her romantically. "You work primarily with victims of trauma, treating post-traumatic stress disorder and related conditions?"

"Yes, that's what I've spent most of my career doing." Bryce nodded.

"Why don't you tell us a little about your methods," Tom suggested. He wanted to get an understanding of exactly what this man did with his patients.

"Okay. Well most sufferers of PTSD struggle to deal with the emotions surrounding the traumatic event that they suffered because those emotions are just so understandingly overwhelming. Because those feelings are so negative and so difficult to cope with, PTSD sufferers can often hamper their own recovery by avoiding anything and everything that reminds them of the trauma. It might be a strategy that helps them to function day to day, but it also limits their processing of the event and thus limits their recovery," Dr. McCracken summarized.

"So, what do you do to help them?" Chloe asked, looking genuinely interested.

Focusing on Chloe, the doctor explained, "I use cognitive processing therapy. I use trauma specific techniques to help victims work through what happened to them and their feelings and emotions surrounding it and help them work toward recovery."

"One of those techniques is exposure therapy?" Tom asked.

"Yes, it is. The primary focus of what I do, or cognitive processing therapy in general, is to help the patient learn to face and understand the trauma they experienced, and the beliefs it has created in them and the emotions that it sparks, so we can decrease the ongoing negative impact it has on their life. Learning to stop avoiding those triggers is a major part of that. Avoiding doesn't solve the problem; in fact, it makes it worse. So, we start by helping the patient to better understand PTSD symptoms and the way that treatment is going to help them. Then we want the patient to think about where they are currently, what are their understandings of why the traumatic event occurred, and the impact it's had on them and their beliefs and feelings about themselves and the world following the trauma. Next, we work on processing the trauma. This is understandably the most difficult part, but it is necessary for the patient to learn to clarify and then modify their distortions in their views of themselves and the world that the trauma created. Once we've done that, we can work on helping them change those so we can improve their quality of life."

"How does the exposure therapy fit into that?" he asked. That's what they needed to know. Had the doctor taken that theory to the extreme and set up the robbery to try to help Hannah overcome her fears?

"Exposure therapy is based on the principle of respondent conditioning. We want to identify the thoughts, emotions, and physiological arousal that accompanies the stimuli that induces fear, then break that pattern by facing the fear rather than running and hiding from it. We usually take small steps toward the greatest fear-invoking stimuli, working through them, processing them, and making sure the patient is ready to move on to the next step. Depending on the condition, generalized anxiety disorder, phobias, obsessive compulsive disorder, or what I primarily deal with, which is PTSD, we might approach things a little differently."

"What specifically do you do to help them learn to face their fears?" Chloe asked.

"Well, there are three types of exposure. One is confronting feared bodily symptoms, such as panic attacks with increased heart rate and shortness of breath that make the sufferer feel like they can't breathe, so we work on calming techniques and how these feelings will pass and are nothing to be feared. Another is confronting the fear of thoughts and memories, where we work on imagining a situation that they fear, and that again these thoughts and memories can be managed and are not anything to be afraid of. And the third, is real-life exposure, where we put the patient in a situation where they must confront their fear-inducing stimuli."

That was what he wanted to know more about. "Isn't that harmful to the patient? Putting them back into a situation where they were harmed and traumatized in the first place?"

"Obviously, it's a case-by-case situation. And obviously, I'm not going to take a sexual assault victim and put them back in a situation where they fear they are going to be raped. But we can work on things such as returning to the location or type of location where the assault occurred, so they no longer fear that place. Or we can work on issues such as regaining intimacy with their significant other that might have been compromised by the assault."

"From what we heard, you like to put your patients in the most dangerous of situations you can to help them overcome their fears," Tom said, watching for the doctor's reaction.

"I have a good success rate," Bryce said evenly.

"One of your patients is Hannah Buffy?"

"Yes. Is this about the robbery at her store?"

"You heard about that?" Tom asked.

"Hannah called me the following morning and asked if we could make an appointment. I have her booked to come in on December twenty-ninth."

"Did you set up the robbery?" he confronted the doctor with their suspicions.

Bryce's eyes grew wide. "Of course not. I would never set up a dangerous situation as a form of therapy without the patient's consent, otherwise it's just going to do more harm than good. In Hannah's case, given her fear of guns, having her held at gunpoint when she wasn't prepared to come face-to-face with a weapon would be extremely counterproductive." The doctor paused and eyed him shrewdly. "I know who you are. You're Hannah's ex-husband."

"You know about me?"

"Of course. I've been seeing Hannah for close to three years now. I know about the home invasion, and I know about what it did to your marriage." The doctor's face now turned sympathetic.

"Did Hannah talk about me? About us?" Tom wanted someone to tell him that Hannah still loved him, and that they could fix the problems in their relationship the assault had caused.

"You know that's privileged. I told you about the gun phobia because I know you already knew about it, given your relationship with her, but don't forget I'm Hannah's doctor, I can't tell you what we spoke about. Hannah is a very special woman, strong and resilient, and I want to see her happy. I want to see her succeed in life. I would never do anything that would prevent that from happening. And pretending to rob her store just to make her confront her fear of guns *would* hamper her recovery, and thus stop her from being happy."

Looking into Dr. Bryce McCracken's earnest face, Tom couldn't decide if he was simply a dedicated doctor wanting to help his patients however he could. Or someone who'd gone beyond the realm of the doctor-patient relationship and developed an obsession with Hannah that ran so deep he would do whatever it took to save her and make her his very own.

∾

10:17 P.M.

She couldn't move.

There were so many hands on her, holding her down.

She tried to fight against them, but there were too many.

And they were so strong.

She was never getting away.

Hannah knew she was going to die here in this room, with her husband watching.

That was the worst.

As those men held her down, their fingertips digging into the flesh of her arms and her thighs as they pulled her legs apart, she couldn't bear to look at him. She could hear his agonized groans and grunts of impotent fury as he tried to break free of his own bonds.

Every time one of the men entered her body, she could hear the chair Tom was tied to thumping and clattering against the floor as he tried to get to her.

Having accepted her fate, she scrunched her eyes shut and tried to block everything out. Tried to put herself in a place where she couldn't feel anything.

The best she could hope for right now was a quick and painless death, but feared her death would be anything but.

She had no hope.

She knew only pain.

Hannah had no idea how long it went on.

Eventually, the pain faded and she became numb.

Then a gunshot sliced through the stillness . . .

Hannah woke with a start.

Her heart was hammering and her body was drenched in an icy sheen of sweat. She was shaking so badly she was making the chair shake with her.

Scrunching her eyes closed, she tried to breathe through her terror.

In through her nose and out through her mouth.

In through her nose and out through her mouth.

In through her nose and out through her mouth.

Eventually, she started to regain control of herself. Her breathing had slowed, as had her heart rate, she still shivered a little, but now it was more from cold as the air met her wet skin than from fear.

She had clenched her hands into fists, clutching the blanket that was draped across her, so tightly that it took a moment for her stiff fingers to uncurl. She flexed her hands, stretching her fingers out wide, then took hold of the blanket again and pulled it up to her chin.

Hannah glanced at the clock on the small table beside her armchair. It wasn't even eleven o'clock yet. It was going to be a *long* night. A very long night.

She eyed her bed. Should she go and lie down, make herself more comfortable and see if that helped her go back to sleep? She hadn't spent a full night sleeping in a bed since the night before the home invasion. She had spent months working on the issue with both Dr. Langley and Dr. McCracken, but she couldn't seem to overcome the fear.

Some nights she would start in the bed, but she always had night-mares and lasted no more than a couple of hours before she woke in a panic. When that happened, she would give up and move to the armchair in the corner of her bedroom. Most nights she didn't even bother attempting the bed.

It was one thing for Dr. McCracken to say that her nightmares couldn't hurt her, that her bed was only an object, that nothing bad was going to happen if she slept in it, but he wasn't the one who felt the fear. She knew that the nightmares couldn't hurt her physically, but they certainly hurt her psychologically. And on the nights when she tried the bed, she always—without fail—had bad dreams. Then she was afraid to close her eyes for the rest of the night, so she didn't sleep. Then she walked around the rest of the day in a fog.

If it was up to her, she probably wouldn't even bother to keep the bed. She never saw herself spending an entire night in one again, but it was easier to have it there in case friends or family happened to come up to her bedroom. It saved a lot of questions. Dr. Langley, Dr. McCracken, Garry, and Tom were the only ones who knew that she usually slept in a chair.

Tom.

He seemed to have taken up permanent residence in her head.

She couldn't not think about him.

At the moment, that kiss was at the forefront of her mind. When his lips met hers, it took her back to the past. To how happy she had been with him, how happy they had been together. At how excited she had been to share her future with him and of all the things they had to look forward to together. Of the deep, passionate, all-consuming love she'd had for him.

That love was still there.

It hadn't gone; it had only been overshadowed by the trauma they had shared.

They had turned their backs on each other, right when they needed each other the most. She couldn't blame Tom for leaving. He wasn't altogether wrong when he accused her of pushing him away. It hadn't been intentional, though. Hannah *had* wanted him there by her side, but not to cosset and protect her, just to encourage and support her. And when he hadn't done that, she had started insisting that he not hover at her side, that he not be with her all the time, that he let her do things for herself.

She had given him the impression that he wasn't wanted.

So, he'd left.

Tom might have been gone from her life for three years, but what she felt for him had remained.

Maybe there was a way to bring it back.

She hoped there was.

Giving up on sleep for now, Hannah stood up, tossed the blanket onto the armchair, and snuggled into her fuzzy pink robe with a teddy bear face on the hood. She headed downstairs to the kitchen, flipping on lights as she went. She'd worked hard to overcome her phobia of the dark, eventually learning not to need the light on all night every night, but after a nightmare, she reverted back to needing the light.

In the kitchen, she set about making herself a snack. She hadn't had any dinner. Her stomach had been all tied up in knots thinking about Tom and the kiss and whether or not it meant that they might get back together or whether he just felt sorry for her.

That was her biggest fear.

To Tom, she would always be a victim. He couldn't help but see her as one after he watched her be gang raped for almost seven hours. She understood that. She just couldn't allow that sort of mentality to be around her. She had fought so hard to overcome the victim label, and she didn't want to go back to that place. She didn't want to be pitied. She wanted to be treated like she wasn't helpless, and she didn't want to be treated like she was fragile and might fall apart if she was handled the wrong way.

She wanted to be treated like the strong, resilient, independent woman that she was.

If Tom couldn't do that, then no matter how much she still loved him, they could never work things out.

And if Tom never admitted he needed help, that he needed to let go of the guilt he felt, that he needed to acknowledge that he had been a victim too, then she didn't think he could ever see her as anything other than a victim.

Right now, the ball was squarely in his court. He could keep pretending that this was just a job and that she was just a victim who needed saving, or he could recognize things for what they were and do something about it.

She really hoped he chose the latter. Because she couldn't allow anything to interfere with her sanity. Most days it balanced precariously between survivor and victim, and it took a lot of effort and work and conscious action to keep herself firmly on the survivor side. And not even for Tom would she allow herself to cross back over to victim.

Hannah was just removing her bowl of oatmeal from the microwave when she heard a sound.

She froze.

Surely, she must be wrong.

But then she heard it again.

Something was definitely moving around out there.

Some*one*.

What should she do?

Should she hide? Should she call 911? Should she try to find a weapon and stay here and defend herself?

Her eyes scanned the kitchen and fell on the utensil drawer. Setting the bowl on the countertop, she armed herself with the biggest knife she could find. Her cell phone was still upstairs on the table beside her armchair, but there was a phone on the table over by the fireplace. She just had to get to it.

She was halfway there when she heard something bump against her door.

For a moment, she was paralyzed with fear.

This could *not* be happening again.

But then, she relaxed.

Tom.

It would be just like him to be patrolling her house, paranoid that if he didn't, this "monster" he believed was stalking her would show up and hurt her.

In a way, his overprotectiveness was a little endearing, but in an even bigger way, it was annoying and even insulting. How many times did she have to tell him that she didn't need to be saved?

Knife still in hand, she stalked to the door, unlocked it, and threw it open, prepared to give him a piece of her mind, but choked when she saw who was standing on her doorstep.

11:28 P.M.

Hannah's house was exactly what he would have expected her to choose. Two stories, painted a fresh, bright white, a big porch, a neat and simple garden with neatly mowed lawns, and big trees that would provide lots of leafy shade in the summertime. It was exactly the type of house they had spoken about owning one day.

Only that day had never come.

As Tom watched her house from his car, he saw a light flicker on upstairs, and then a moment later, one downstairs.

Hannah couldn't sleep.

They'd both had issues with sleep following the home invasion. For months afterward, every time he closed his eyes, he was back in their bedroom, reliving that hell over and over again until it threatened to send him insane.

Part of him wished that he had never woken up. That the blow to his head had kept him unconscious throughout the entire ordeal.

But it hadn't.

The men who had broken into their home that night had waited for him to regain consciousness before beginning their assault on Hannah.

They had *wanted* him to watch.

To have to sit there, tied to a chair, helpless, and watch every despicable thing they did to his wife.

The look of horrified resignation on Hannah's face as they ripped off her clothes was forever seared into his consciousness.

As were her anguished cries, muffled by the hand over her mouth, as those men had forced themselves inside her.

Tears had streamed down her pale face, trickling down onto the pillow.

As he tried relentlessly to free himself so he could rip those monsters to shreds with his bare hands, he had watched, unable to tear his eyes away, as blood began to pool between her legs, staining their white sheets a vivid red.

Tom remembered the sounds of Hannah dragging in a harsh breath as the men wrapped their hands around her slim throat and squeezed, cutting off her air supply, then letting go just as she began to pass out.

They'd laughed while they tortured her.

That sound was almost worst of all.

By the time he had been freed and gotten to her, she was in shock. She was covered in blood—not all of it her own—and it had smeared all over his naked chest as he had gathered her limp form into his arms. Her eyes had been open and vacant, staring at nothing as he rocked her and whispered a string of meaningless consolations into her tangled auburn hair, that were more for his benefit than hers, because he didn't think they penetrated her shock-fogged brain.

Hannah had been shaking so badly that, by the time the paramedics had arrived, the cops had collected every blanket in the house for him to wrap around her, which had done nothing to still her tremors. The EMTs had sedated her and her haunted eyes had finally fallen shut.

He had refused to release Hannah, holding her the whole drive in the ambulance to the hospital. Once there, he had refused treatment until he knew for sure that Hannah was okay. And even then, he had had the doctor stitch the gash in his head in Hannah's hospital room, as he kept a vigil at her bedside, holding her hand.

Concerned that there might be further swelling in her throat from the damage it had sustained, and dealing with internal injuries, Hannah had been kept in the hospital for several days. Even before she was released, as soon as she was allowed out of bed, she had started sleeping in a chair.

According to Garry Smith, she still did.

Tom wished he could wipe all that fear away.

If he could, he would.

In a heartbeat.

His attention suddenly snapped to Hannah's front yard.

Was that movement?

A shadowy figure was heading straight for Hannah's front door.

He was out of his car and moving before he even knew it.

As he was running across the street, he saw light spill out as Hannah's door opened, and he could see that the figure he'd seen in her yard was none other than Garry Smith.

For a moment, he faltered.

Was he overreacting?

Had Hannah and Garry lied that they had broken up and were, in fact, still a couple?

Was this just some midnight rendezvous?

As soon as he reached her door, he knew it wasn't.

Hannah's face was a mask of fear, and in her hands, she clutched a large knife.

Tom wasn't sure whether Garry was a threat to Hannah or not, but he was going to play things carefully just in case the man was dangerous.

"Everything okay here?" he asked. His hand hovered over the butt of his gun, but he didn't pull it out.

Hannah's eyes darted in his direction, and he saw her relax a little, but she didn't loosen the death grip she had on the knife.

"Everything's fine," Garry said, but didn't take his eyes of Hannah.

The look on the man's face was borderline crazy. He was obsessed. He couldn't let Hannah go. Tom just hoped he wasn't going to turn violent. "It's pretty late, Garry, maybe we should let Hannah get some sleep."

"She was up. I didn't disturb her. I would never disturb her. She doesn't sleep much. I'm always telling her she needs her rest." Garry spoke like he and Hannah were still a couple. Perhaps in his mind they were.

"She was up," Tom said agreeably, "but she shouldn't be. Like you said, she doesn't sleep much, and when she does, it's always in a chair. She needs to rest."

"When you leave, I'll take her to bed," Garry said.

Hannah stiffened. She was so pale, Tom was afraid she was going to faint. But she didn't. Instead, she pulled herself together. "I don't need you to take me to bed, Garry. I can take care of myself. It's late. You should go home now."

Garry wavered, apparently not wanting to upset Hannah by not doing as she asked, but clearly not wanting to leave. "I'll call you tomorrow?"

"No," Hannah said firmly. "I told you that it was over between us. You shouldn't be calling me."

"Someone robbed your store. I just wanted to make sure you were safe," Garry said in a whine.

"You don't need to worry about that, Tom and his partner will find the people who did that," Hannah told him.

Garry grew angry at that. "Tom, your ex-husband. Since when did he ever help you?"

The man whirled around to face him, and Tom was glad to have his attention away from Hannah. "You need to leave, now, Mr. Smith. Or I *will* be placing you under arrest." Trespassing was the best he could do. It wasn't a crime to turn up at your ex-girlfriend's house in the middle of the night. The most Garry Smith would get was a fine, but Hannah could apply for a protective order, and if Garry was the one who had set up the robbery, then he would find that out and send him to prison.

"*You* should leave. You and Hannah are divorced. You hurt her when you left. Just leave her alone; she doesn't want to see you." Garry was devolving right before his eyes, and Tom knew then and there that the man was a threat and should be treated as such.

Keeping Garry's attention focused on him, he took a step closer. "Hannah ended things with you, Garry. She has asked you to leave. You have two choices: you can do as she asked, or I can arrest you and have you removed from the property in handcuffs."

With a frustrated growl, Garry turned, and Tom thought he was going to accept defeat and leave, but then he turned back, his fist swinging through the air. Instead of connecting with his jaw, Garry's fist sailed past when he ducked, then Tom grabbed the man's arm, twisting it up behind his back, causing Garry to yelp.

Whipping out a pair of handcuffs, he snapped them on then pushed the man down onto his stomach. With Garry restrained, Tom turned his attention to Hannah who still stood, rooted to the spot, her wide eyes staring in disbelief at the man whom she'd dated, whom she'd trusted.

She still held the knife.

"Hannah," he said softly, taking a cautious step toward her, not wanting to startle her.

Slowly, her eyes moved to meet his, and some of the shock and fear left them, replaced by gratefulness, and something else he couldn't quite put his finger on.

"Here, let me take that." His hands closed around hers, finding them ice cold, and gently eased the knife from her grip, setting it down on the counter, then taking hold of her hands again, rubbing them vigorously between his own, trying to warm them. "Are you okay?"

"Yes," her voice trembled. "Tom, if you hadn't been here—"

"Stop," he held a finger to her lips to silence her. "I was here. And even if I wasn't, you would have handled yourself just fine."

~

11:56 P.M.

"Are you sure you're all right?" Tom asked, probably for the twentieth time in the last twenty minutes.

Hannah nodded, still unable to comprehend everything that had just happened.

Her ex-boyfriend, Garry Smith, had just been dragged from her house—in handcuffs—screaming that he loved her and always would, and that he would do anything to make sure she was safe. For the first time since Tom had mentioned the possibility to her, she actually believed that someone had set up the robbery at her store because of her.

How had she not seen that Garry was obsessed with her?

She hadn't been in love with him, but she had certainly liked him. He was definitely someone she would choose as a friend. He was sweet, gentle, and kind. She'd thought he was completely harmless.

Although she had known that his feelings for her ran deeper than hers did for him, she thought he'd taken the breakup well. He'd been disappointed but seemed to understand that she didn't want a future with him. She had thought he would just move on. Find someone else, someone who wanted the same things out of life he did, someone who would love him as much as he loved them.

"You're not hurt?" Tom asked. Even though he knew that Garry had never laid a hand on her, he took hold of her by the shoulders and held her at arm's length, his eyes travelling her body in an assessing search. When he saw no injuries, he crushed her against his chest.

Hannah didn't fight him. Instead, she just rested her head against Tom's strong chest, wrapped her arms around his waist, and leaned against him. For once, his overprotectiveness had worked in her favor. If he hadn't been here tonight, she didn't even want to think about what might have happened. She didn't really think that Garry would have physically hurt her, but she also didn't think that he would have been watching her house in the middle of the night, and then turned up at her door because he saw that she was up.

He could have hurt her.

There would have been no one here to stop him.

But there had been.

Tom.

Not only had he been here, but he had told her that even if he hadn't, he believed she would have known how to handle the situation. That he had that much faith in her made her heart swell in her chest till it filled to bursting. Maybe he didn't think she was a weak, helpless, victim who needed saving.

She wanted to believe that so badly, but she couldn't let her heart rule her head until she knew for sure where he stood.

"What were you doing here tonight?" she asked, gently tugging herself out of his arms.

"Watching your house." Tom released her slowly, letting his hands trail down her arms before finally letting go.

"Is this the first night you've done that?" She already knew it wasn't, but she wanted to hear him say it.

"No. I slept in my car across the street last night, as well."

"Why?"

"It's my job."

So, they were back to that again. Hannah sighed and went to the kitchen, putting the knife she had armed herself with earlier away, and dumping the cold gluggy oatmeal into the trash. She was getting sick of Tom and his mixed messages. After everything he knew she had been through, it seemed so unfair that he would be here toying with her emotions for no good reason.

"It's my job, Hannah, but that doesn't mean I don't want to be here."

She turned around to find him standing just a couple of feet behind her, his brown eyes brimming with emotion.

"When I saw it was Garry at your door, at first, I was so jealous. I thought you were still with him, and you'd just lied to protect my feelings."

Jealous?

That was a good sign, right?

It meant he still had feelings for her.

"Then when I saw the fear in your face, I knew that you'd been telling the truth, and I knew that if he'd been watching your house, it wasn't good. I was scared, Hannah. I don't ever want to see you hurt again."

Was that all this was?

He was being nice to her, hanging around, protecting her, not out of a sense of responsibility to his job, but as a sense of responsibility as her ex-husband. He blamed himself for the home invasion, so he was going to do whatever he had to, to make sure that this time she didn't get hurt.

Which did hurt.

She'd thought there was more to it.

Tired and overwhelmed by the night's events, she just wanted to go upstairs to her room, curl up in her chair, let herself have a few minutes to cry and break down, then try to get some sleep. Not that she would.

"I'm going to bed."

When she moved to brush past him, he grabbed her arm, holding her in place. "I said something wrong. What?"

"Don't worry about it," she said dismissively.

"I'm trying, Hannah."

"To do your job. I get it. I really do. I'm sorry if I'm somehow making that difficult."

He released her and huffed out a frustrated breath. Then grabbed her shoulders, pulled her close and kissed her. This time, the kiss was soft and gentle and tender.

When he pulled away, big fat tears began to roll down her cheeks. She wanted this. She hadn't realized just how much. In the last three years, she had pushed all thoughts of Tom to the back recesses of her mind. It had been too painful. But now that he was back and standing here in her kitchen at midnight, she knew that she wanted him back. She just wasn't sure it was what he wanted.

Tom reached out and caught her tears on his thumb, brushing them away. "Don't cry."

"I can't help it," she sniffed.

"I know. You should go and try to get some more sleep." The backs of his fingers still rested against her cheek, and his voice was impossibly gentle.

The prospect of being alone in her house all night wasn't a pleasant one. If it hadn't been so late, she might have even considered calling her parents or one of her sisters to ask about spending the night. "Yeah, okay. Thanks for being here tonight, Tom. I'll see you out."

"I'm not going anywhere. You don't think I'd leave you here alone after what happened, do you? I'll sleep on the couch."

Her mouth opened, ready to shoot back a retort at the over confident way he declared that he was spending the night, but then she snapped it shut. Having Tom downstairs on the couch might help her to actually get some sleep, and maybe even sleep without nightmares. "Thanks, Tom."

"No arguments?" He looked surprised, like he had been all ready for a fight.

She gave him a half smile, "No arguments."

"So, the girl can be taught after all." One side of his mouth quirked up in a half smile of his own.

"I guess she can; I'll grab you some blankets and a pillow."

"I'll get them, just tell me where they are."

"Upstairs hall closet, grab whatever you want."

While Tom ran up the stairs, taking them two at a time, Hannah picked up the bottle of sleeping pills from the kitchen counter and tipped two into her hand. She was just screwing the lid back on when Tom returned, his arms filled with blankets, a quilt, and two pillows.

"You're still taking sleeping pills?" he asked.

"It's the only way I can sleep through the night. Or at least, mostly through the night." She had been taking Silenor since the assault. She'd tried going off it and just sleeping on her own, but she usually stressed herself so much about whether she would fall asleep, whether she would stay asleep, and whether she would have nightmares, that every time one of her doctors tried taking her off it, they ended up putting her back on it within a couple of weeks.

"Don't feel bad, Hannah," Tom told her, beginning to make up the couch. "If you need the pills to sleep, then you need them. There's nothing wrong with that. If your doctors didn't want you to take them, then they wouldn't write you a prescription."

Tom's words made her feel better. She'd forgotten he had that effect on her. It was probably the main reason she had pushed him away. She trusted his opinions of her, and when it felt like he thought she was a victim who couldn't cope without him, then it made her feel like that had to be true. "You can sleep upstairs, if you want, in one of the guest bedrooms," she offered.

"Thanks, but I'm fine down here." From the look on his face, she got what he meant without him having to say it out loud. He wanted to be downstairs in case there was any more trouble.

Feeling safer and more at peace than she had in three years, Hannah poured herself a glass of water, took her pills and headed for the stairs. "Goodnight, Tom."

"Goodnight, Hannah."

CHAPTER
Five

December 22nd
7:56 A.M.

Tom actually felt well rested this morning. It wasn't as though he had gotten a lot of sleep last night, between the hubbub with Garry Smith, half expecting another monster to turn up at Hannah's door, and knowing that she was upstairs asleep in her bed—well, her armchair— he had laid awake most of the night. But knowing he was making progress with her was like a weight had been lifted off his shoulders.

Things with Hannah were still pretty precarious, teetering between growing closer and pushing each other away again. He wanted to make his focus solving this case, but whenever he was around Hannah, he couldn't help but kiss her. Tom knew he was sending her mixed signals, and he knew it needed to stop.

He'd been going to talk with her this morning, but she had been asleep when he'd left and she needed the rest so he hadn't wanted to wake her, but he couldn't put it off any longer. The longer he waited, the more he continued to tell her this was his job, the greater the chance that he would lose her again. He kept saying the wrong thing because he was trying to make keeping her safe his top priority. Thinking back, that might have been why he lost her in the first place. He couldn't bear the thought of her in pain, so he had constantly tried to wipe it all away, to take it from her and make it his own. Hannah hadn't wanted that, she had accepted quicker than he had that what had happened was a part of them forever. They couldn't take it away, but they could learn to live with it.

He hadn't been able to accept it, so he had lost the woman he loved.

Now, he wanted her back. And he actually had a chance of making it happen.

Tom was sure that Hannah wanted to reconcile just as much as he did.

If he was wrong, if he asked and she said she wasn't interested in getting back together, then at least he would know.

A week ago, getting back together with Hannah had been the last thing on his mind. When he'd walked into her jewelry store four days ago, he'd thought that maybe they could both walk away from this case with closure. Now, closure was the furthest thing from his mind. He didn't want closure; he wanted his wife back.

"Coffee," Chloe announced as she set a takeaway cup down on his desk and shrugged out of her coat, scarf, and gloves.

"Thanks."

"I can't believe Christmas is only three days away." Chloe pulled off the reindeer beanie she'd been wearing since October and set it on her desk.

He couldn't either. He hadn't decorated for Christmas since the last one he'd celebrated with Hannah. He went to his family's gathering, exchanged gifts, sang carols, and ate too much Christmas dinner, but his heart was never in it. Obviously, Hannah's wasn't, either. She didn't have a tree or a single Christmas decoration up in her house. And he knew how much she loved the holidays. When they'd lived together, she had decorated every single room in their house, filling it to the brim with Christmassy decorations and festive fairy lights. The look of joy on her face when she discovered a new decoration she just had to add to her collection was priceless.

Hannah's Christmas Eve ritual of leaving milk and cookies out for Santa and carrots for his reindeer always made him laugh. As soon as she would fall asleep, he would sneak downstairs to eat the cookies, drink the milk, and gnaw on the carrots. In the morning when they woke up and went downstairs to open their presents by the tree, Hannah would always make a big deal out of pretending Santa had been and loved her homemade cookies. Her joyful laugh filled their home and his heart, making the day the single most perfect day of the year.

He wanted that joy for her again.

For *both* of them.

And he knew the only way they could find it was together.

They were so close. If Garry was the one who had set up the robbery in an attempt to draw Hannah back to him, then they had him in custody. All they needed was some proof to keep him locked up.

"How's Hannah after what happened last night?" Chloe asked.

"She was still asleep when I left, but she'll be fine." Despite what Hannah apparently thought, he had always seen her as the strong woman that she was. "She was shocked and upset, and I think it threw her that she hadn't seen Garry for who he really was, but if this was what it took to find that this was all because of her ex, then I think she's glad it happened—scary as it was at the time."

"It was lucky you were watching her house or things might not have worked out so well."

"It was," he agreed. He honestly wasn't sure if Garry would have physically hurt Hannah or not, but regardless, he was relieved he'd been there before things even had a chance to get out of hand and turn violent. "I spent some time this morning looking into Garry Smith."

"Oh, yeah?" Chloe arched a brow. "We didn't look into him too deeply when we spoke with him before. He doesn't have a criminal record."

"No, he doesn't. But he *does* have a psychiatric one."

"How did you find that out?"

"I spoke with his sister."

"The sister?"

"She was upset to hear about him being arrested and quick to tell me that he's unbalanced, and that this isn't the first time he's gotten a little too obsessed with a girlfriend. It's not even the second or the third. Hannah is the fourth woman that Garry has gotten out of line with." Although it had scared Hannah and himself, he was glad that last night had happened. If it hadn't, Garry's actions would have escalated.

"What did he do?"

"The first incident was back when he was in high school. He latched onto a girl after a school dance. They had never even dated, but he built up this relationship between them. He started leaving gifts and notes in her locker, followed her around. After he started turning up at her house at night, her parents threatened Garry's parents that if they didn't make him stop, they were going to press charges. His parents took him out of school and homeschooled him for the remainder of his junior year and his senior year."

"When did he strike again?"

"College. Same sort of thing, only this time he had been dating the woman. When she ended things, he started stalking her. At first, she thought it was fairly harmless and he would eventually lose interest and move on. When he didn't, she ended up transferring to a different school to get away from him."

"She didn't press charges?" Chloe asked.

"No, she didn't. She tried, but stalking cases are so hard to prove. When cops talked to him, he said that it was all just a big misunderstanding, and since Garry hadn't done anything threatening and the girl hadn't been hurt in any way, the cops never took it further."

"He escalated with the third one?"

"He did," Tom agreed. "The third one was a few years later. He was in his mid-twenties, working at a bank, and the woman was a colleague. They dated for about a year before things ended. She thought they ended amicably enough. And for the first couple weeks, it seemed like they did. And then the gifts and flowers started coming. Garry was still posting all over his social media accounts like they were still a couple. He started turning up at her apartment in the middle of the night, like he had with the others, he never made any attempts to get inside, he would just sit and watch the house. Then one night, he broke in."

"Did he hurt her?"

"Not badly. He was convinced they were still a couple. Tried to get into bed with her. When she fought him off, she received some minor injuries."

"What happened? He doesn't have a criminal record, so he wasn't arrested."

"They made a deal that if he got some psychiatric help that no charges would be filed against him. He did. He spent a few months at an in-facility treatment center, then came out, he takes medication and sees his psychiatrist once a month."

"Doesn't seem to be helping," Chloe muttered.

"It looks like Garry could be a viable suspect. He knew Hannah's store, and he could have gotten in when she wasn't there to plant the listening device. He has a reason to want to scare her, and he knows that Hannah has suffered a trauma before. He probably thought if he shoved her right into the middle of another one, he could get her to come back to him. He knew Hannah saw a therapist and maybe thinking they had that in common, he decided to fight harder to keep her than he did with the others." The thought of another man obsessed with Hannah got his blood boiling and his protective juices flowing.

"We can't be sure yet that Garry was the one who set up the robbery," Chloe reminded him. "We haven't ruled out Bryce McCracken yet."

~

8:43 A.M.

She was just about to get up and walk out the door, unable to spend another second in this place without driving herself crazy, when the door swung open.

"Thanks for coming down here, Hannah," Special Agent Luckman smiled at her.

"Are you okay?" Tom asked, his eyes assessing but emotionally empty.

He was back in cop mode. She couldn't take much more of this. Hannah understood that this was his job, that he was an FBI agent, and that he solved crimes and saved people. It wasn't that she didn't want him to do his job or that she didn't understand his desire to protect her, but she couldn't keep spending time around him when he kept switching between the Tom she had known before and the one who was like a stranger.

"Hannah?" he prodded, when she didn't answer.

"Yeah. Fine. What did you want to ask me about?" She wished Tom had still been at her house when she woke up this morning; she'd liked falling asleep knowing he was close by. When his partner had called her to ask if she would come and answer some questions for them, she had reluctantly agreed. The sooner they ended this, the sooner she and Tom could sit down and talk.

"I don't want you to worry about Garry," Tom said. "He's going to be charged, and if he's the one who organized the robbery, then we'll find out, and he will be charged with that, as well."

"Is Garry going to be kept in jail?" she asked.

"He'll probably be out on bail," Tom replied.

So, there would be nothing stopping him turning up at her house again. And if Tom wasn't there the next time, she might not escape unscathed.

"He won't have a chance to hurt you again." Tom said it so confidently, she believed him. "His family is aware of his problems. He has a history of being unable to let go of relationships. They're going to make sure he doesn't come near you again. And you should take out a restraining order; if he does turn up at your house again, his bail will be revoked."

"Yeah. Okay," she agreed, although it didn't seem like a piece of paper was going to protect her much if Garry came back. And if his family knew that he was a danger to women, why hadn't they done something about it? She and Garry had dated for a little over a year. She'd met his parents and his sister, and never once had they mentioned anything to her about him being unbalanced. And how had she not noticed that he was unbalanced? He had seemed so perfectly normal. She never would have pegged him for having any sort of mental health issue.

"It'll be okay, Hannah. I won't let him hurt you." Her Tom was back. The fire in his eyes, the protectiveness in his voice—this was who Tom was, and if they were going to get back together, she was going to have to learn to accept it. She might not want a husband who was a guard dog, but she could put up with it if it was what Tom needed to do.

"All right," she agreed, putting her trust in Tom. "What do you want to ask me? Is it something about Garry?"

"No, we want to ask you about Bryce McCracken," Tom's partner informed her.

"Dr. McCracken?" she repeated. Tom had asked her about him before. If they wanted to talk to her about him again, they must really think there was a chance he was behind all of this. He had been her doctor for nearly three years now; he'd helped her a lot. She would never be where she was right now if it wasn't for him. She had loved Dr. Langley, and when the woman had retired shortly after she and Tom had divorced, she had considered giving up therapy. But she'd known she wasn't ready yet to take that step and asked her doctor for a recommendation, and she'd been introduced to Dr. Bryce McCracken.

"Do you like him?" Chloe Luckman asked her.

"Yes."

"Your sessions with him have helped you?"

"Yes. A lot."

"He said you'd called him after the robbery."

"Yes. I wanted to work on my phobia of guns." Hannah had been deliberately avoiding looking at the agents' waists where she knew their guns were, but now her gaze dropped there, and she felt a shiver rocket through her. The six men who had ambushed Tom and broken into their home had tortured her mercilessly with their weapons. They had ground them into her temple and her forehead—leaving her with bruises far more substantial than the one from the other night—and laughed while they did it, pretending they were going to shoot her. Then they had pushed the barrel of the gun inside her and laughed again, like it was all some big joke to them. They had run the cold metal of the gun all over her body, asking her where she wanted them to shoot her first. She had believed she was going to die that night, and if it hadn't been for one of their neighbors, she and

Tom would have. Her gaze now riveted on Tom's weapon, Hannah pulled her bottom lip in behind her front teeth and chewed on it nervously.

"Do you want us to take our guns out of the room?" Tom asked.

She did—desperately—but she knew that if she wanted to overcome her phobia, she had to start somewhere. Neither Tom nor his partner were a threat to her, so here was as good a place as any to start. Deliberately, she ripped her gaze from his waist to his face and calmed her ragged breathing. "No, its fine."

"What are some of the things you and Dr. McCracken have worked on?" Chloe asked.

"You don't have to answer that, Hannah," Tom inserted. "It's up to you. Your sessions with your therapist are privileged."

She didn't have anything to hide, and she didn't believe that her doctor was in any way involved in the robbery, so she was happy to tell them whatever they wanted to know—at least the basics. They didn't need to know all the details. "We worked on my feelings to do with the assault. Techniques to help deal with the panic attacks. Dealing with my fears of the dark and being alone and sleeping in a bed. I wasn't very successful with the bed one."

"How did he help you overcome your fears?"

"It wasn't really about overcoming them; it was learning to manage them. I'm probably always going to be jumpy alone in my home at night, but I got to a place where I can do it even if I'm not one hundred percent comfortable with it. We did exposure therapy. With my fear of the dark, we worked at it in steps. At first, he had me try not having every light in the house on. Then we worked on being in the dark for short times. Then we worked up to longer times until I got to the point where I could last throughout an entire night without having to have a light on in the room."

"You were happy with his methods?"

"Yes."

"He never pushed you to try something you weren't comfortable with?"

"I wasn't *comfortable* with any of it, but no, he never pushed me harder than I could cope with."

"You never worked on your phobia of guns with him before the robbery?"

"I think we might have talked about it early on, but it wasn't as pressing to me as my fears of the dark and being alone and learning to deal with the panic attacks. Those things affected my everyday life; guns didn't. I never came in contact with them. It wasn't until the robbery and I realized that Jeff and Vincent could have died because I froze up that I decided I had to do something about it."

"Did he ever do anything to make you feel uncomfortable?"

Tom stiffened as his partner asked that, his guard dog side was out in full force again.

"He never made me feel uncomfortable. I like him."

Tom relaxed, and asked, "What do you know about him?"

"He mostly works with victims of PTSD. He loves apples and eats them all the time, and he recently got divorced. Other than that, he's just a good doctor. He's helped me a lot."

"Do you know any of his other patients?" Chloe asked.

"Not really. I might say hello and exchange pleasantries with them if we're waiting together in his waiting room, but that's about it. Why do you think he might have done this?" She couldn't hold back her curiosity any longer.

"Families of some of his patients have filed complaints about his methods," Tom informed her.

"The exposure therapy?"

"Yes. He took it to the extreme a few times and ended up causing his patients more harm than good."

"What did he do?"

"One of his patients was a young woman who had been raped while jogging in the park with her dog. She hadn't been able to exercise since and had put on a substantial amount of weight. Her dog had tried to fight off her attacker, and the rapist had killed him. She hadn't been able to go near a dog since. Her family finally convinced her to seek help and she did. At first, things were going well. She worked on her inability to be around dogs and got to the point where she got a new puppy. Then he pressured her to agree to let him set up a fake assault. After working with Dr. McCracken, she'd been able to go back to exercising, taking to the gym rather than jogging. She was happy with her progress. Her family was happy with her progress. But the doctor wanted more. He convinced her to go jogging and told her he was going to set up a fake assault. He did, and it set the woman back in her recovery."

Hannah frowned. "That's taking the exposure therapy too far." If Dr. McCracken had set it up for a group of men to pretend to break into her home in the middle of the night, it would have brought everything back. It wouldn't have helped her. At all.

"That's what her family thought."

"Were there any other instances like that one?"

"There were a couple of others. All since his wife filed for divorce," Tom replied.

"But he had their permission, right? I mean, he might have pressured them to say yes, but they *did* say yes. He never asked me about working on the gun phobia by throwing me into a fake armed robbery, so I really don't know that he would have had anything to do with it." She didn't think that Dr. McCracken was involved, but her relationship with him had certainly been soured by what she'd just learned. She couldn't continue to see him as her doctor; she'd have to find a new therapist.

"Maybe he's trying to make a name for himself in the psychiatric world by trying methods that are extreme. Or maybe he feels some sort of attachment to you for some reason, possibly because you bear a striking resemblance to his ex-wife. I don't know," Tom said, "but if he's involved, we'll find out."

She nodded, feeling so overwhelmed. A week ago, she had just been going about her everyday life, trying to make it through the holidays, focusing on work. Now she'd been held at gunpoint, discovered that the man she'd dated was an unbalanced stalker, and the therapist she trusted was more interested in himself and his career than helping his patients. What was going to happen next?

～

12:20 P.M.

. . .

Hannah yawned, a huge face-splitting yawn. She was really struggling to keep her eyes open today, which was weird given she'd had a better night's sleep than she had in the last three years.

The feeling of being overwhelmed was still there—and no doubt the cause of the drained and exhausted feeling that swamped her—but she was making strides to overcome it. She had started looking for recommendations for a new therapist. She had called a home security firm to see about having an ungraded system installed at her house, and she was back at her store determined to finish the list of stolen stock.

It was a tedious task because she had to go through every single item of jewelry left in her store because she couldn't be one hundred percent sure exactly what Jeff and Vincent had put into the safe. She had a printed list of inventory beside her and was working her way through the boxes where she had stacked the jewelry crossing each item off on the list when she confirmed it was still here. She was bored and tired and finding it difficult to concentrate, but she'd put it off long enough. And it wasn't like she had anything else to do, so she was going to sit here and work on it until it was done.

Her stomach grumbled loudly.

She was starving; she hadn't eaten anything yet today. When Tom's partner had called and asked her to come to their office, she'd left immediately, and when they were finished questioning her, she'd come straight here. She hadn't eaten dinner last night either, and she was kind of iffy on whether or not she'd had lunch yesterday.

Maybe she should stop and grab some lunch now, come back to this later.

It was tempting.

But if she stopped this close to being done, she wouldn't want to come back and finish it later. And she really had to finish. She needed to know exactly what was gone so she could file her insurance claim, and Tom and his partner wanted to know.

Hannah sighed.

No more procrastinating. It shouldn't take her more than another hour or so to finish going through everything, then the task would be done, and she could go get something to eat, then maybe head home and grab a nap.

She was working through the box that contained some of her most expensive stock, stuff that was *always* kept in the safe overnight, when she froze.

Something was missing.

Something that shouldn't be.

A heart-shaped five carat diamond ring worth around $65,000 wasn't there.

It should be there.

How could it have gone missing?

It would have been in the safe the night of the robbery.

There was *no* way that Jeff and Vincent wouldn't have put it in there. They packed up most nights, and they'd always put it in the safe before.

It had been in the safe.

She was the only one who had the code.

She hadn't given the robbers the code, so the robbers couldn't have taken it.

So, where was it?

It had to be here somewhere.

Standing quickly, she hurried to the safe. It was probably still in there. Maybe it had somehow fallen and was lying unnoticed on the floor. That seemed unlikely; the safe was only five feet by five feet, and lined with shelves, which she kept perfectly organized. But where else could it be?

Punching in the code, Hannah threw open the door and dropped to her knees, running her hands along the floor, searching for the missing ring.

She found nothing.

Next, she worked her way up, shelf by shelf, both looking and feeling to see if the ring was there.

It wasn't.

It was gone.

It should be in the box. There was no way the robbers could have taken it. It was impossible. It was in the safe when they were here. Someone had taken it *after* the robbery. Which meant there were only two people who could have done it.

Jeff or Vincent.

She'd given them the code. She'd had to. There was no way she could risk another robbery, and her phobia of guns causing her to freeze up again, so she had given the code to both her employees, intending to change it once Vincent moved on. Never again would she be the only one who could access the safe.

Why would Jeff or Vincent have stolen one of her rings?

There was only one reason she could think of.

They had set up the robbery and stolen the ring to pay the men they'd hired, hoping she would just assume it had been stolen the night of the robbery.

Tears pricked the backs of her eyes. How could she not have seen that one of her employees was psychotic and out to get her? Probably the same way she hadn't see that Garry was psychotic and out to get her.

Hannah had never felt so betrayed in her life.

It seemed like rather than working with a therapist on overcoming her phobia of guns, she needed to work on learning how to more accurately read people.

At least now she knew who it was. Jeff and Vincent were the only people with the code to her safe, and they had access to the store, so they were the only ones who could have snuck in here and taken the ring following the robbery.

She had to call Tom and tell him.

As she walked out of the safe, she sensed the man was there even before she saw him.

She opened her mouth to scream, but he was on her before she could make a sound.

He was big.

So big.

And wearing a balaclava.

That was good, right? If he didn't want her to see his face, there was a chance that he didn't want to kill her.

He held a knife in his hand and he grabbed hold of her arm, yanking her up against his chest, clamping his free hand over her mouth and holding his knife to her neck.

This had to be one of the men who'd held a gun on her the other night.

Now that she knew that they didn't just want her merchandise but her, as well, it was so much more terrifying.

What did he want from her?

Who had hired him?

Why had one of her employees hired him to rob her store and then come back to get her?

"You're pretty," his voice whispered in her ear. His breath through the thick black material that concealed his face was hot and stinky.

Hannah shivered; she was so scared. If this man raped her, she didn't think she could deal with it.

"So pretty," he drawled. He moved the knife so the tip punctured the skin on her cheek and trailed it down, around her chin, along her neck and down onto her chest.

The cut was shallow but Hannah could feel a small trickle of blood seeping out. The knife was above her heart. Was he going to kill her? She didn't understand. What did Vincent or Jeff want from her? Robbing her store was one thing. That could easily be explained away by greed, but sending someone here to cut her, to possibly rape and kill her, made no sense.

Whatever the reason, she wasn't going down without a fight.

"I bet men throw themselves at you all the time." The masked man pressed the knife deeper into her flesh, cutting through her rose and lilac striped cashmere sweater and into the skin of her left breast. "I bet you take advantage. Use them to get what you want and then dump them once you have it." He pressed the knife deeper still, and she cried out beneath his hand. "Not so pretty now, huh?" he chuckled as he gouged a hole in her breast.

He was going to torture her before he raped and killed her.

She had obsessively taken self-defense classes since the home invasion, learning every single technique she could in case she was ever in a position where she needed to use them.

And now she was.

Lifting her right leg, she kicked backward and to the side, aiming for and connecting with the man's knee.

He yelped in surprise and released her.

Hannah darted for the door. It was the middle of the day and only three days before Christmas. There would be lots of people at the mall. She just had to get their attention and help would come.

She hadn't caused her attacker as much damage as she'd hoped, and he lunged at her, tackling her and sending them both sprawling to the floor. As soon as they were down, he flipped her onto her back and sat on her stomach, pinning her down. Hannah didn't give up. She reached up and gouged her finger into where she believed his eye was. Her aim must have been spot on because he howled a string of profanities and backhanded her across the face so hard she saw stars.

By the time they cleared, he'd slapped a piece of duct tape over her mouth. "I didn't like that," he growled, digging his finger into the wound on her breast.

She screamed, the sound muffled by the tape.

She was so scared she had almost moved beyond fear, to a distant empty place her mind had gone to before.

She was disconnecting.

With quick efficient movements, the man turned her over onto her stomach and pulled her arms behind her, securing her wrists together with layer after layer of tape. He did the same with her ankles. Her attacker put something over her eyes, and she felt him tie it behind her head.

Bound, gagged, and blindfolded, she was helpless against him.

Completely helpless.

As he picked her up, her mind descended into the peace and serenity of shock.

～

1:03 P.M.

As he walked toward Hannah's jewelry store, Tom wondered what he should get her as a Christmas gift.

That they would spend Christmas together was already a given in his mind. They might not spend the whole day together. He might not share Christmas lunch with her, and they both might be busy with their respective families, but he had no doubt that they would see each other.

He wanted to give her something special, something meaningful, something that showed her how much he still loved her and how much he wanted them to find a way to work things out. He wasn't sure yet exactly what that would be, but he had no doubt he would think of something. He still had time.

He had an hour before he had to be back at work, and he hoped he and Hannah would have enough time to talk—both personally and professionally. He wanted to let Hannah know that this wasn't just a job and that he wanted more. Tom also wanted to let her know about the listening device they'd found in her office, and find out whether either Garry Smith or Bryce McCracken might have had access to her store to leave the bug.

In his hands, he carried two cups of soup from Hannah's favorite store, a peace offering of sorts. He wanted to apologize for his repeated claims that everything that had happened the last few days was all just a job. It wasn't. And he couldn't keep using that as an excuse to keep a barrier up between the two of them. If he and Hannah were going to find a way to put their relationship back together, there couldn't be any more hiding from each other. He couldn't complain that Hannah shut him out when he did the exact same thing.

The mall was busy with people everywhere, and Hannah's quiet store seemed out of place. He wished that none of this had happened, that no one had set out to target her, that she had never been held at gunpoint, that her store hadn't been robbed, that she wasn't missing out on business during the busiest shopping season of the year.

Although . . .

If none of that had happened, though, they wouldn't have been thrown back together. He was selfish enough to be thankful for anything that brought them back together. He just wished Hannah hadn't been hurt in the process.

He opened the door to her store and movement through the open workroom door caught his attention.

"Hannah? It's Tom."

No answer.

He was immediately on edge.

His gut said something was wrong, and he *always* trusted his gut.

Without hesitating, he dropped the cups of soup, pulled out his gun and ran through the store. As he entered the workroom, he saw blood on the floor, a man in a black balaclava, and no signs of Hannah.

"FBI, freeze!" he yelled at the man.

The man was close to the door to the office. If he got through it, he could escape out the back door.

That was *not* going to happen.

Tom had his gun trained on the man, and he would use it if he had to. The man hadn't moved and appeared to be weighing up his options.

Apparently deciding it wasn't worth trying anything stupid, the man put his hands up.

"Down on the ground," Tom ordered.

The man complied, getting down on his knees, then lying on his stomach, his arms out above his head. He knew the drill. This man had been arrested before.

Cautiously, he crossed the room, keeping his gun trained on the man as he pressed a knee into his back and reached with his free hand to snap a handcuff around his wrist, pulling the man's arm back, then putting his gun away in order to reach for the man's other arms to finish cuffing him.

With the man restrained, Tom yanked off the balaclava, "Where is she?"

A sullen, pock-marked face pouted back at him. His left eye was red and swollen. Hannah had fought back.

"Where is she?" he repeated, fighting the urge to pummel the man he knew had hurt Hannah.

"The safe," the man muttered.

Calling in backup, Tom darted to the safe. "Do you have the code?"

"No."

He had to figure it out. He had to think. What would Hannah choose? She was smart enough not to do her birthday. She had named her store with a nickname he had given her, because that reminded her of him and the happy times they'd shared. Would she choose a date related to the two of them?

Tom tried their wedding date.

It didn't work.

Next, he tried the date they'd met.

Again, it didn't work.

He tried the date that he'd proposed.

Another failure.

He was starting to panic. The red light on the keypad was flashing at him, mocking him. He wasn't familiar with the particular system Hannah used and was afraid that if he kept putting in wrong numbers, the system would just shut down altogether.

That couldn't happen.

He *had* to get in there.

The blood on the floor told him Hannah was hurt. He just didn't know how badly. She could be bleeding out on the other side of the door. He had to keep it together.

Sunkissed Jewels.

Her store's logo was printed on the door of the safe.

Sunkissed.

He had first called her that when they had spent their first vacation together. They'd been at the beach, chasing each other through the waves. He'd carried her on his shoulders out to the deep water, then tossed her in. She'd paid him back by staying under and not coming up for air for an impossibly long time. Afterward, they'd laid in the sand, the sun drying their wet bodies, tangled in each other's arms. In the sunlight, the red in Hannah's hair had shimmered and shone, and as her head on his chest had tilted up to look at him, the freckles across her nose and cheeks had looked like little kisses from the sun.

That day.

That was the code Hannah had chosen.

Tom knew it even as he punched in the numbers, and the keypad rewarded him by changing its light from red to green.

He was in.

He quickly spun the handle and swung open the door.

Hannah was lying on the floor of the safe. She was bound, gagged, and blindfolded.

She lay on her side and he could see that her sweater had been cut, and the edges were covered in blood. A line of blood ran from her cheek, down her chin, along her neck and disappeared under her sweater.

Her sweater had a hole right above her heart.

The man had cut her breast.

As she heard the door to the safe open, she tried to wiggle backward, away from him, he heard her whimper through the tape on her mouth.

"It's okay, Hannah; it's me," he said as he dropped down at her side.

At the sound of his voice, she stilled, and he saw her sag back against the floor in relief.

Supporting her head in one hand, Tom pulled off the blindfold. Hannah's eyes were watery, but she wasn't crying. As carefully as he could, he pulled off the tape covering her mouth. Hannah flinched as it took off a layer of skin with it.

"Are you all right?" he asked, taking her face in his hands and searching her eyes for answers.

"Mmhmm." She gave a small nod. "Did you get him?"

"I did." His heart was still hammering in his chest. That man could have killed her. And what had he had in mind for her if he hadn't been interrupted? "Hannah," he leaned down and pressed his forehead to hers.

"I—I'm okay," she assured him. She was trembling, but she was holding it together. Just.

"I'll go get something to cut the tape." He gently laid her back down, and she winced as the movement jostled her wounds.

Leaving her was difficult, even for a moment, but he had to get her free. Her attacker still lay where he'd left him, and Tom glared at him as he ran past and into Hannah's office to find a pair of scissors to cut away the tape that bound her. He hated that man. *Hated* him. But at least now he could get the answers he needed.

Back in the safe, he sawed through the tape at her ankles, then sat Hannah up, propping her against his body as he leaned behind her and freed her wrists. He rubbed at her hands to restore circulation, then turned his attention to the wound on her chest. "How bad is it?"

"I don't think it's too deep."

Grabbing the strip of cloth the man had used to blindfold her, Tom supported Hannah against his bent knee and pressed the material to her chest, stemming the flow of blood from her wound. Sirens filled the air, and he relaxed a little. Hannah was okay, and now that they had the man who had attacked her, she was safe, as well. There was nothing left standing between the two of them reconciling.

"Tom?" Chloe called out a moment later.

"In the safe," he called back.

"You got him," his partner appeared behind him.

"Good timing," he said.

"Is she okay?"

"She is," Hannah replied, sitting herself up straighter and grimacing as it caused pain. "Tom, go and find out who he is."

"Hannah ..." He didn't want to leave her.

"Please," she begged. "I need to know."

"Fine." He'd do it for her; he would do *anything* for her. He helped her move backward so she could rest against the wall, then lifted her hand and held it to her wound. "Keep pressure on this."

She squeezed his hand before taking over keeping pressure on the cut. "Thank you," she whispered. A single tear escaped and rolled slowly down her cheek.

He kissed her forehead then very reluctantly left the room, leaving Hannah with his partner. Cops were dragging Hannah's attacker to his feet.

Tom saw red.

The man had hurt Hannah. He deserved to be hurt a million times worse.

But this man was only the middle man. He wasn't the one they needed. They needed the one who'd planted the bug—the one who was after Hannah.

"Who is it?" he demanded, stalking across the room.

"Who's what?" the man asked, but Tom could tell by the look in his eyes that he knew exactly what was being asked of him.

"Don't lie to me and don't play games," he growled, getting right up in the man's face. "Who paid you to hurt Hannah?"

The man squirmed.

"Who?" Tom held his face millimeters from the man's.

"I don't know his name."

"Then how did he find you?" Why did nothing on this case go smoothly? They had one of the men who'd committed the robbery at Hannah's store, they had confirmation someone had set it up on purpose. But the only man they had in custody didn't even know who had hired him.

"Through a friend."

"The other man who held up the store a few nights ago."

The man nodded. "But he ran a couple of days ago. We were supposed to get the ring and then disappear, but he took the ring and ran." The man's face grew bright red, and he vibrated with anger.

"What ring?"

"He promised us a ring that was worth more than fifty grand."

So, it *was* an inside job, someone who knew what Hannah had in stock. "Why did you come back here?"

"He asked me to. Said he'd get me a ring of my own. All I had to do was come here and scare her. I was just gonna leave when you showed up."

"Do you have a phone number for this man?"

"He uses a different one every time."

Burner phones. "Is he young or old? Any accents? Anything you can tell me about him from talking to him?"

"He sends texts."

Tom groaned. Of course he did, because nothing went smoothly in this case. "Take him away," he told the cops. As they led the man away, Tom noticed he was limping. Hannah must have gotten in a blow to his knee. His heart swelled with pride. She never gave up, she was the ultimate fighter.

"Did he tell you who it is?" Hannah asked when he returned to her side.

"No, I'm sorry. He said he doesn't know."

"It's Jeff or Vincent. I gave them the code after the robbery. One of them went in and stole a ring. I was going to call you and tell you when the man attacked me." She began to chew on her bottom lip, and he couldn't help but smile. She was so adorable when she did that.

"We'll figure it out," he promised as paramedics joined them in the small, cramped room. He should probably move back and give them more space to work, but he didn't. The fear of turning up here to find a masked man and blood on the floor, and then seeing Hannah tied up and bleeding, hadn't left him yet. It wouldn't for a long time.

While one EMT began to check Hannah's vitals, the other shot him a look. "I'm going to have to remove her top to check her injury."

"Okay."

"Tom," Hannah raised a brow at him.

"You already used up your one ask-me-to-leave-the-room pass. You don't get another one."

For a moment, Hannah looked like she was going to argue, but then she turned to the medic. "It's fine, go ahead."

As the medic cut away her damaged sweater, Tom saw the continuation of the long shallow cut that started on her cheek, and a much deeper wound on her left breast that was still oozing blood. How dare that man mar Hannah's beautiful breasts. The desire to pummel him until his face was a bloody, unrecognizable mess was overwhelming.

"How bad is it?" he asked, when the medic was finished examining it.

"Needs a couple of stitches."

"You'll do that here," Hannah said, not asked.

"If that's what you want," the medic agreed.

"It is."

"You should go and see a doctor within the next day or so if you're not going to go to the hospital," the medic cautioned.

"Okay," Hannah agreed noncommittally.

"I'll make sure she does," Tom inserted. He expected Hannah to complain, to inform him that she didn't need anyone to take care of her, that she could take care of herself, that it was none of his business whether she decided to go and see a doctor, and that he'd overstepped his bounds.

But she didn't.

She said none of that.

She just smiled up at him.

~

3:15 P.M.

He hoped he hadn't scared Hannah *too* much.

He only needed her scared enough that she would seek comfort and solace in his arms, but so far it didn't seem to be working.

Why hadn't she come to him?

He didn't understand it.

He knew she had a phobia about guns. The fake robbery at her store should have been enough to send her running straight for him.

But it hadn't.

He had waited patiently, trying to give her time, not wanting to take things further unless she left him no other choice. Still, she didn't come.

When it became clear that he *didn't* have any other choice, he had reluctantly upped the ante. He had sent one of the men who had committed the robbery back to Hannah to scare her a little more.

He wasn't pleased to hear she'd been injured.

That wasn't part of the plan.

The man was just supposed to scare her, maybe tie her up and leave her. He wasn't supposed to cause her physical harm. He would have to be clearer about that next time. It couldn't happen again.

Even with one of them taking things too far, finding those two men had been a serious stroke of luck. They had been greedy enough to do what he'd asked in exchange for the ring. Which was the perfect payment because it didn't even cost him anything. Hannah would just assume the robbers had taken it and add it to the list submitted to the insurance company, so she would be reimbursed for it, as well. A win-win.

As great a plan as he'd had, it still didn't seem to be working.

So, he'd come here.

He was at a loss; he didn't know what to do next. He couldn't risk Hannah being physically hurt again, so maybe this would show her how much she meant to him.

Carefully, he picked the lock on the back door of Hannah's house. He knew where she lived, but he'd never been to her house before. Well, he had never been *inside* her house before. He'd been here lots of times.

Just watching the house. It made him feel closer to her here. And if he was lucky and he came by in the summertime, he might see her sitting in her backyard in a bikini, lying on her lounge with a book in her hands.

He loved those days.

He'd sit and stare at her, transfixed, imagining what it would be like to touch her, to kiss her, to run his hands all over her body, to put his hands inside her body, to be inside her, to come inside her. Those times he watched her usually ended with him masturbating, because she got him so hard he just couldn't help it.

He would have her.

He wouldn't allow any other outcome.

How could he be without her?

He dreamed about her every night. She drove him wild every time he was in the same room as her. She consumed his thoughts during the day and his dreams at night.

He had to have her.

He had to.

He'd thought she would be his by now.

Maybe she would be if it wasn't for that FBI agent.

He knew who the man was. He knew *everything* about Hannah Buffy. He knew that her full name was Hannah Jade Buffy. He knew that she had been born on October 31st, the second of three daughters to Joel and Freya Buffy. He knew that while her older sister Rachel had been the sporty one and her younger sister Bethany was the academic one, Hannah had been the artistic one. She might be artistic, but she was smart, too, and had been a straight A student throughout school. He knew that she loved to swim, read, and ski, in addition to making jewelry. And that Special Agent Tom Drake was her ex-husband.

He knew about the home invasion.

He knew that it had destroyed her marriage.

He knew that when she was suffering the most, her husband had walked out on her.

He knew that it had been three years since they'd last seen each other.

Only now, it seemed Tom was back, and it looked like he wanted Hannah.

Well, that was not going to happen. Tom Drake had had his chance with Hannah, and he had tossed her away. Now it was his turn. And he would never, ever let her go. Not for anything. No one was going to get in the way of him getting what he wanted. No one was going to stop him from having Hannah for his very own. No one. And if anyone, including FBI agent Tom Drake, got in his way, then he would kill them.

Hannah would be his.

As soon as she knew how much she meant to him and how he wanted to make her the very center of his universe, she would be happy to belong to him. She would know that he would make her happiness his top priority. She would know that his love for her was all-consuming.

She would know that soon.

Maybe she already knew it, and she just needed that little push to overcome her fears and turn to him. To learn that being strong and independent was a good thing, but so was letting the man who loved you more than life itself take care of you.

These gifts would show her how he felt about her.

Chocolates, because Hannah was the sweetest person he had ever met, in a heart-shaped box, because she and she alone owned his heart. And a bouquet of forget-me-nots—for true love and because he would never forget her—tulips—red for undying love—and violets—blue for faithfulness. He had chosen all of them especially for her. He hoped she appreciated them.

He tiptoed through her kitchen. Even though he knew she wasn't here, her house filled him with a sort of reverence. He set the gifts on her kitchen table where she would be sure to find them when she returned home.

He wanted to stay, to be here waiting for her, but he couldn't. That would startle her and he didn't want to do that. She had to be the one to come to him, and she would.

Perhaps even today.

After what had happened earlier, she would be scared and shaken and in need of comfort and support. Who better to give it to her than him?

She would come.

She would.

He was sure of it.

~

4:40 P.M.

"Ready to regroup?" Chloe asked.

Tom looked up from his computer where he'd been running background checks for the last hour. He hadn't wanted to leave Hannah; he didn't want to be away from her right now. When the paramedics had finished with her at the store, she had allowed him to drive her to one of her sisters' houses so she wouldn't be alone and someone could keep an eye on her following the attack since she wouldn't go to the hospital.

He knew she was all right and he knew she was being well taken care of and he knew he was going to go back and watch her house tonight, but that didn't loosen the pull that wanted to draw him back to Hannah's side.

But he had a job to do, and he was going to do it. He had to make sure that Hannah was safe. He couldn't stand the thought of her in danger again, of her being hurt again. He kept picturing the bloody gash on her smooth white skin. That would not happen again.

Focus on his job.

That was what he had to do right now.

"You want to go first?" he asked his partner.

"You can."

"The man who attacked Hannah today is Tristan Hinkle. He's twenty-seven and has a lengthy criminal history. Assault and battery, domestic violence, a kidnapping. Started with fights at bars, then the cops were called to his house several times after he beat his girlfriend. He'd be sent to prison, and she kept taking him back every time he got out. When she finally decided she'd had enough, he kidnapped her."

"How'd he do so little time for the kidnapping?"

"Took a deal to a lesser charge and pled guilty. He'd been out of prison for about two months before the robbery at Hannah's store."

"Who was his partner?"

"Troy Abbadakka. Also twenty-seven, he grew up with Tristan, they lived across the street from each other, went to school together, and got into bar brawls together. Troy has also been in and out of prison. Mostly snatch-and-grab robberies. He'd stake out ATMs, wait for someone to withdraw cash, then follow them, hit them over the head, and run off with their bags. He was out for about four months before the robbery."

"So, he had plenty of time to set up the plan with whoever orchestrated the robbery."

"He did. And according to Tristan, it was Troy who was the one who had contact with the man who wants to hurt Hannah. I looked into whether either Tristan or Troy spent time in prison with Warren Maloney or his cousin, and I didn't find any connections."

"We know the robbery at Hannah's store wasn't related to the others," Chloe reminded him.

"I know. I just wanted to confirm to make sure. According to Hannah, a ring worth around sixty-five grand was missing. Tristan confirmed that whoever hired them was going to give them a ring as payment. Which means it was an inside job. We're looking at either Jeff Shields or Vincent Zimmerman."

"Jeff was shot," Chloe said.

"What better way to throw suspicion off himself than to be injured? If we didn't know about the ring, we wouldn't even have been looking at him. And Hannah thought that he'd left the building. He was in the back room; he could easily have gotten away, but he stayed."

"Hannah stayed, too."

"Because she wanted to try and get Vincent out before the men got to him. But Jeff could have left. He didn't. And not only didn't he leave, but he didn't even stay in the office. He went into the workroom where Hannah and Vincent were being held at gunpoint," he said.

"To save Hannah."

"Right. The timing is suspicious. He stayed out of sight until right when Hannah was going to be shot, then he bursts in to save her."

"I guess you could look at it that way," Chloe agreed.

"But we looked into both of them at the time of the robbery and neither of them had criminal records; so what did you find?" They had split the work—he looked into the two men who robbed Hannah's store, and Chloe looked into Hannah's two employees.

"Jeff Shields is fifty-four, never married, no children, but he comes from a big family. He has nine brothers and sisters and over fifty nieces and nephews. It seems like he's pretty involved with his extended family, and has had some of his siblings' children come and live with him at various times for various reasons. He has worked at the jewelry store for the last thirty years. When Reginald Thames sold the store to Hannah, he stayed on."

"Doesn't really sound like the kind of man who would want to hurt her," Tom reluctantly acknowledged.

"No, he doesn't. Besides work and family, he also volunteers at a homeless shelter and works with underprivileged kids."

That caught his attention. Hannah had volunteered at a homeless shelter for as long as he remembered. She also always donated some of her wages to help underprivileged kids. Coincidence or something more?

"What?" Chloe asked, reading the look on his face.

"Hannah does, too."

"A possible connection," she agreed.

"What about Vincent? He had only been working for Hannah for a month. Is that long enough to become obsessed enough with her to want to hurt her? Especially given that he doesn't have a criminal record."

"*Vincent* Zimmerman doesn't have a criminal record, but *Charles* Zimmerman does," Chloe beamed at him, her brown eyes glowing with excitement.

"Who's Charles Zimmerman?"

"Vincent's brother."

"You think he might be involved?"

"In a way."

"You think that Charles somehow coerced Vincent into helping him? Or somehow took advantage of him? Or that both brothers were involved?"

"In a way."

"Chloe," he growled with frustration. He got that this was all new to Chloe and that the thrill of solving a case got her all excited. But this wasn't a game to him. This was Hannah's life. He wanted answers. Now.

"You know how Hannah said that her friend Ellen's husband had died fairly recently? Well, what she didn't say was that one of Ellen's sons had died, too."

"She probably didn't think it was relevant."

"She probably didn't; she would have no reason to."

"But you think it is?"

"Vincent and Charles were twins. They were inseparable up until high school, then they headed down different paths. Vincent wanted to be a doctor, and he studied hard. He didn't spend much time with the other kids, he didn't go to parties, and he didn't date. All he did was study. Charles was more into the party scene. His grades started to slip when he started drinking, and it got out of control. He had numerous drunk driving offenses, and he wasn't even legal drinking age when he died. Charles was a violent drunk, particularly with his father. Gavin Zimmerman was a competitive shooter, so he owned several guns. A few times, Charles got a hold of them and threatened his parents and brother. The police were called a few times and Charles was sent to rehab, but it wasn't very successful."

"That's all interesting background on the brothers, but what does it have to do with this case? Charles Zimmerman is dead, and he was the brother with the problems."

"Gavin and Charles died in a car accident. Gavin had been sick; he'd had several heart attacks in the couple of years before his death, so the cause of the accident was deemed to be Gavin having a heart attack at the wheel, losing control and causing the car to crash."

"You think it was something else?" So far, Tom had no idea where his partner was heading with this.

"Vincent was in the car at the time, too. The bodies were pretty badly messed up. The car hit a brick wall, which crushed the entire front of the car. Gavin and Charles were unrecognizable, and . . ."

"And you think Charles Zimmerman saw an opportunity to change his fate," he finished, finally catching on. "It was really Vincent

Zimmerman who died in the car accident, and Charles decided to assume his brother's identity."

"If Charles didn't successfully complete his rehab program, he was facing prison time. Maybe he found the perfect way around that."

"That is the craziest idea I've ever heard." Tom shook his head in disbelief. "And you thought I was seeing things that weren't there when I first suggested the robbery at Hannah's store wasn't committed by the same men who'd been robbing jewelry stores. We have *zero* proof that Hannah's employee, Vincent Zimmerman, is really Charles Zimmerman."

"We had no proof that your theory was right either, but it was. There's someone who would know which son died in the accident."

"Hannah's friend and neighbor—Ellen Zimmerman. If you're right, then she's helped cover this up. She went along with it, even coming up with a story about why Vincent had dropped out of pre-med and needed a job at the jewelry store. Why would she do that?"

"She lost her husband and one of her boys. The only one that survived was facing prison time; maybe she couldn't face any more loss."

"Let's say you're right. Let's say that Charles stole Vincent's identity, but none of that explains why he would want to hurt Hannah." Right now, as interesting as Chloe's theory was, that was all he cared about. He wanted to know who was after Hannah before they managed to hurt her again.

Or worse.

If someone was obsessed with her, then when they made their play for her and realized that she was never going to reciprocate their feelings, then there was a chance that they would kill her.

The thought of Hannah being gone paralyzed him.

He couldn't let that happen.

He wouldn't.

They needed to talk with Vincent or Charles Zimmerman and Jeff Shields. They needed answers and they needed them now.

∽

8:59 P.M.

. . .

Sometimes she was too stubborn.

Hannah knew that.

Like tonight, she *would* have preferred to spend the night at her older sister Rachel's house, but when her sister had offered, she'd said no, she would be fine at home on her own. Then when Rachel dropped her off here, she *would* have preferred that her sister come inside and stay the night, or at least stay for a while, but again when her sister had offered she had said no, that she would be fine here on her own.

Her desire to prove that she wasn't a victim, that being raped hadn't turned her into a different person, that it hadn't destroyed her, that she was a survivor, was sometimes stronger than she could manage. It made her feel like she needed to keep proving herself over and over again. She had to show everyone that she was okay, that she wasn't fragile, that she wasn't going to break.

Tom wasn't the only one who had treated her like a delicate porcelain doll after the assault. Her parents and sisters had, too. Hannah didn't want anyone to see her that way. Those men hadn't destroyed her. She had bounced back; she was resilient, and she wasn't going to let anyone crush her.

But maybe it was time to find a balance between being strong and being human. And humans needed other humans. Over the last three years, she had emotionally distanced herself from everyone. It was hard to know that the people she loved hurt because she hurt, and there was only so much hurt she could cope with. As much as she claimed she was strong and she could handle everything all by herself, some days she didn't want to. Some days, she wanted someone there to give her their strength when her own faltered. It was exhausting pretending she had everything under control all the time, that she was strong enough to handle everything, that she could do it all herself.

She wanted a break.

She wanted Tom.

She just had to be positive he wanted her, too, and for the right reasons.

She couldn't take him back if this was just about him and his need to save her because in his mind he failed her last time.

Hannah waved to Rachel as her sister backed down the driveway and pressed her other hand to her chest. The deeper wound on her breast ached, and the stitches pulled when she moved or turned. It was going to leave a nasty scar. Despite the violence of her assault, she hadn't been left with any physical scars, and the prospect now of having one, and on her breast, was upsetting.

She knew it was just a scar, nothing more than a mark on her skin. But it was on her breast. How was Tom going to feel about that? Would he still find her attractive? And even if she and Tom never got back together and she ended up with someone else, would it impact how they saw her?

There was no point in worrying about it now. She and Tom weren't even close to sorting things out, and other than him, she couldn't really ever see herself with anyone else.

Hannah opened her front door and walked inside.

Her house looked so empty.

Well, it wasn't empty. She had lots of beautiful furniture, and she had spent ages searching for and choosing just the right pieces. There was art on her walls, and photos and vases of flowers and other accents on the tables. There were throw cushions on her sofas, and all the other little things that made a house a home.

But there were no Christmas decorations.

There were only three days until Christmas, but you couldn't tell it by walking inside her house.

Christmas had been her favorite holiday for as long as she could remember, but the last few years, she just hadn't had the heart or the energy to decorate her home and immerse herself in the joys and fun of the season. She still had all the decorations she had been collecting since she was a little girl packed in boxes in her attic, and maybe one day soon, she would feel like getting them out again, but for now, she was okay with just enjoying Christmas day with her family and nothing else.

As she flicked on lights and made her way through the dining room to the kitchen, she remembered the fun she and Tom had had celebrating Christmas together. He had enthusiastically embraced her all-encompassing love and childish joy around the holidays, going along with the traditions she hadn't let go from her childhood. He had made Christmas all the more special, and . . .

She lost her train of thought the moment she stepped into the kitchen.

Her back door stood slightly ajar.

On her kitchen table, there was a bright red box shaped like a heart and a bouquet of flowers.

Someone had been inside her home.

It had to be whoever was targeting her.

Were they still here?

Slowly, she began to back out of the house.

As she walked, she scanned her surroundings, searching for signs of movement or a person hiding in the shadows. She couldn't see anyone, but that didn't mean that they weren't there.

Her hand fumbled around inside her bag, then her fingers curled around her phone.

Who should she call?

911 or Tom?

She was scared and she wanted to call Tom, but she wasn't sure she should. She wasn't quite sure exactly where she stood with him right now. He kept telling her that he was just doing his job, and while she knew he still had feelings for her—maybe even still loved her—he had made it very clear that his job was his number one priority at the moment. He had said that this was just a job so many times that she had gotten the message.

Hannah was dialing 911 as she unlocked her front door and stepped outside, but as she turned around, she saw Tom's car.

Relief washed over her.

Shoving her cell back into her bag, she ran toward him. She wasn't even halfway there when he got out and came running to meet her.

"What's wrong?" he asked, his brown eyes glowing with concern.

"Someone was in my house. He left me gifts. On the kitchen table."

He reached for his gun. "Is he still there?"

"I don't think so." She already felt so much better having Tom here, she might be able to take care of herself, but this went beyond that. Tom was an FBI agent; he knew what he was doing.

"Go wait in my car, lock the doors," Tom ordered as he started toward her house.

No way was she waiting out here on her own. What if the man who left her gifts was still around? What if that was his plan? Wait for her to be alone and unprotected, then make his move. "I'm coming with you," she said as she hurried to catch up.

"Hannah," Tom groaned.

"I'm not staying out here on my own," she said firmly.

"Fine. Then at least stay behind me."

That she was happy to do.

Keeping close to Tom, they crossed her front lawn. She had left the front door open, and Tom cautiously entered, holding an arm out to keep her in place as he scanned her front hall and the dining room to their left. When he saw nothing, he moved into the house, heading for the kitchen. Hannah followed. She didn't think that there was anyone in here, because if there was, they had already had their chance to grab her, and she was, presumably, what they wanted.

Once Tom had cleared the kitchen, he paused at the table, studying the gifts the man had left her. Eventually, he tore his gaze away and ordered, "Stay here and I'll check the rest of the house."

This time she didn't argue, just scrunched herself into a corner and waited for him to return.

"Nothing looks disturbed up there," he announced when he walked back into the room a couple of minutes later. "I'll have you check later to confirm that you don't think he touched anything. I called the FBI's ERT unit to come and dust for fingerprints, but we know it was one of two men."

Vincent or Jeff.

She still couldn't believe one of her employees was doing this to her. It didn't make sense. She didn't understand.

"You all right?"

She blinked and Tom was standing in front of her.

"Hannah?"

Drawing on reserves of strength she didn't know she had left, she nodded. "Yeah. I'm all right. A little shaken up to know he was here in my home, but I'll be okay."

"You will," he agreed.

Tom kept saying that. She had spent these last three years thinking he believed she was weak and helpless, but it seemed she'd been wrong. Maybe he really did see her as strong. Hannah wanted to rest against his sturdy chest. She wanted him to wrap his arms around her and hold her up. She wanted to lean against someone, even if it was just for a little while.

"Hannah," Tom's voice had gone soft, gentle, without the cop tone, "we need to talk."

They did.

She knew that.

But maybe this wasn't the time.

Maybe Tom was right.

Maybe his focus did need to be his job right now.

Whoever was intent on torturing her had already set up an armed robbery at her store, sent someone to terrorize her and leave her bleeding and tied up, then broken into her home and left her gifts. What would they do next? She didn't want to die and she didn't want to live in fear. She needed Tom to find who was after her and stop them.

"Not now," she said. "Later. I know that you're here to do your job. Are you going to stay here again tonight?" Hannah couldn't keep the longing out of her voice and didn't bother to try.

"Of course." Tom sounded all business again.

"Do you need anything from me right now?"

"No. ERT will dust down here for fingerprints and take the gifts."

"I'm going to go to bed. Just call me if you need me."

Part of her thought that Tom would follow her or ask her to stay, but he didn't.

He let her go.

Part of her *wanted* him to follow her or ask her to stay, but it was better this way.

Job first.

At least with Tom here, she might actually sleep well again tonight.

She appreciated his presence more than she could express right now.

Hannah paused at the door. "Thanks for being here, Tom."

"Always."

CHAPTER

Six

December 23rd
6:36 A.M.

As she walked downstairs, Hannah didn't know what to expect. Would
Tom still be there? Had he already left for work? If he had, when would
she see him again?

She wanted to see him.

She wanted him to stay.

And she was trying really hard not to get her hopes up too high.

Although that goal flew out the window when she walked into the
kitchen and found Tom standing at her stove wearing a pair of sweat-
pants and nothing else.

She might have drooled a little at the sight. And not because she was
hungry for breakfast.

"You hungry?"

Hungry?

At the moment, she couldn't really think.

All she could do was stare at Tom.

She really had missed him so much.

"Hannah? Breakfast?"

"Yes," she pulled her robe tighter around herself and went to sit at the table. "You making French toast?"

"Mmhmm," he nodded, dipping a couple of pieces of toast into the bowl and then putting them into a frying pan.

"Your special recipe?"

"Yep."

She had tried so many times to make French toast the way Tom did, but she just couldn't seem to get it right no matter how many times she tried, and no matter how many times she adjusted the quantities. She knew he used eggs and milk, adding cinnamon, vanilla, sugar, and maple syrup. She knew all the ingredients, but she just couldn't get it right.

"Breakfast is served." Tom set a plate down in front of her.

"These are so good," she said as she took a bite. "How are they this good?"

"I'm a good cook."

She laughed at that. French toast was about the only thing Tom could cook. She took another bite and another, each mouthful was so fluffy and light and perfectly sweet. Her eyes closed as she savored another bite; it was like eating little pieces of heaven. "No matter how many times I try, I can't make mine taste like yours. How do you make them taste so good?"

"Secret family recipe."

"One you want to share?" she asked hopefully.

"Nope." Tom grinned at her. His whole face relaxed when he smiled, and she liked seeing him like this. She'd missed it. Those last few months before they divorced had been anything but relaxing.

As they ate, they lapsed into a comfortable silence. She'd missed Tom cooking her breakfast. When they'd still been married, he'd always cooked her breakfast on his days off. They'd usually eat in bed, then take a long hot shower together before getting up to start their day. She had missed so many things about him. But now he was here, and they actually had a chance at reconciling.

When they were finished eating, Tom gathered up the dishes, rinsed them and loaded the dishwasher. He no longer looked relaxed. His work face was back.

"How's your chest feeling this morning?"

"It's all right," she assured him, although it hurt whenever she moved. She didn't want to tell Tom that; he'd only worry.

"I want to check it before I go to work," he informed her.

Hannah wasn't embarrassed for Tom to see her bare chest. They'd been married, after all, and he'd seen her naked lots of times before, but she didn't want to reinforce Tom's penchant for being her protector. "I can clean the wound myself."

"Why do you have to argue with me *all* the time?" Tom frowned.

"I don't want to argue with you," she said quietly. Give and take. Tom needed to protect and take care of her so he didn't feel useless, she needed to take care of herself so that she didn't feel helpless, but there had to be a middle ground. If they wanted to work things out, then there *had* to be. "Okay. Thank you for offering to check it out for me."

Tom looked surprised by her sudden change of heart. "And we need to have it checked out by a doctor tomorrow," he added.

He was pushing his luck. "It's Christmas Eve tomorrow."

"I'm sure we can get you an appointment."

She was giving in only because she knew the wound did need to be checked by a doctor. And because she loved Tom. And if taking care of her made him happy, then she could let him do it. Maybe it wasn't the worst thing in the world to have a husband who wanted to protect her and look after her, as long as he knew that she could do those things for herself. "Fine. So, how's the case going?" She changed the subject.

"We're looking into Jeff and Vincent, but you know them. Which one of them do *you* think could have set all this up?" Tom sat back down at the table across from her.

"I have no idea. I would have said neither. I've known Jeff for almost three years. He worked at Mr. Thames' store, and he seemed to like him."

"Did you ask him to stay on or did he ask to stay on?"

"I think he asked, but it might have been Mr. Thames' idea. It was so long ago, it's hard to remember. Either way, I was happy to have him."

"Have you had any troubles with him?"

"No. Never. He's been great. Any time I'm sick and haven't been able to make it in, he's filled in for me. And he often stays late to pack up and clean so I don't have to do it. It's hard running a small business on your own. I don't have the resources to hire a lot of employees, and having one that is really supportive has been a godsend."

What she'd said made it sound like Jeff Shields was out as a suspect, but Tom's serious face was troubled. "So, Jeff made a point of helping you and spending time around you."

"I guess," she agreed, even though it seemed to be putting a bad spin on things.

"When did you buy this house?"

"About eighteen months ago. I rented an apartment for a while after we broke up. Then when my business started to really take off and I could afford to buy, I got this place."

"Did you know Ellen Zimmerman before?"

"No; we met the day I moved in. She brought around a casserole and introduced herself, offered to show me around the neighborhood. I liked her. She invited me to dinner the following night and I went. Ellen and Gavin and I had a great time and we were firm friends by the end of the evening." Although she tended to keep her distance from people since the assault, Ellen was so lighthearted, although perhaps a little shallow, and that made spending time with her easy and relaxing and even a little freeing. She could just sit back and relax and not worry about anything but having fun.

"What about Ellen's sons?"

"What about them?"

"Vincent works for you. Did you know Charles?"

"Yes, I'd met both of her sons before. Vincent was away at college studying pre-med, but I think the shock of his father and brother's deaths kind of hit him hard and he took a break. That's why he was working for me. Charles had some alcohol problems. I had to call the cops a couple of times when he pulled out one of Gavin's guns and threatened his family."

"Would you say you knew the sons well?"

"No, not well. Like I said, Vincent was away at college, so I'd only met him a couple of times before he came to work for me. And Charles spent most of his time either drinking or hungover. Why the questions about Charles? He's dead; he can't have anything to do with this."

Tom looked like he was debating whether or not to tell her something. He must have decided to because he reached across the table and took her hand. "Chloe suggested something that sounds crazy but might possibly be true."

"What?"

"She thinks there's a possibility that Vincent might really be Charles. That it was Vincent who died in the accident, but Charles decided to assume his identity, get out from under the charges that were going to send him to prison if he didn't complete his rehab."

That was the single most crazy thing she had ever heard.

It couldn't be true.

It couldn't.

How could it?

People didn't just assume their dead brother's identity in real life. That was crazy movie stuff. There was no way that Charles could pull off pretending to be Vincent—the brothers were too different. And Ellen. She would know that it was really Charles who had survived. Why would she go along with that? Simple answer was that she wasn't.

"Charles was an alcoholic. I've never seen Vincent drink. Ever."

"Doesn't mean he doesn't. Or maybe the accident was a wake-up call. The push he needed to stop drinking."

"You really think Vincent isn't really Vincent?"

"I don't know. We're going to speak with Ellen this morning. Maybe that'll help us clear things up. Is there anything that you can remember that happened during the robbery that would make you suspicious of either Vincent or Jeff?"

She tried to put herself back in her store on the night of the robbery, replaying the events over and over, trying to focus on the details, but there was nothing that occurred to her that she hadn't already told Tom. "I'm sorry. I can't think of anything else."

"That's okay." Tom still held her hand and squeezed it, his thumb brushing backward and forward across her knuckles. "I lied, Hannah."

Like magnets, his eyes held hers, and she couldn't look away. "About what?" she whispered.

"It's not just a job. Nothing about you is just a job. I've kissed you twice now; you should know that you mean something to me."

She had known that. She had always known that, but she had needed to hear him say it.

"When this case is over," Tom continued, "we need to talk."

That Tom looked every bit as anxious and unsure as she had felt the last few days was immensely reassuring. They both wanted to find a way to fix what had been broken between them, but neither of them was quite sure how to do it, or quite sure that it was what the other wanted.

But now, she knew.

They still had a lot they needed to sort out, but they would.

She didn't doubt that.

And she could wait until Tom and his partner had found and arrested whoever was stalking her.

There was one thing she couldn't wait for.

Tugging her hand free from Tom's, she ignored the surprise and hurt that flashed through his eyes, then she stood and walked around the table.

It didn't seem fair that he had kissed her twice, but she hadn't kissed him once.

She was going to have to change that.

~

9:12 A.M.

Hannah had kissed him

Tom was finding it difficult to think about anything else.

When he had told her they needed to talk and she'd just sat there looking at him, his heart had dropped. He had been sure that she didn't want to reconcile, that she was just trying to think of a gentle way to let him down.

When she had pulled her hand out of his, he'd felt like his world was crashing down around him. Until these last few days, seeing Hannah again, he hadn't realized how much he still loved her, how strong his feelings still were, and how much he wanted her back.

But he did.

And he would do whatever it took to make it happen.

He had been about to tell her that when she had stood, not to leave the room as he had first thought, but to come to him. To kiss him.

In that moment, he'd known that everything would work out. It might be a lot of work, and it might take some time, but he and Hannah would get back what they had lost. They were already making progress. Although she had initially turned down his request to check on her wounds from yesterday, she had then backed down, and allowed him to clean and tend to the cuts, which looked clean and like they were already beginning to heal.

Now he was so much more motivated to end this case. Today, hopefully.

"She's coming," Chloe said as they heard footsteps on the other side of the door.

They were at Hannah's next-door neighbor Ellen Zimmerman's house, waiting to talk with the woman, who he hoped was going to confirm that Vincent was really her other son Charles, or that Vincent had some reason why he might want to go after Hannah. He didn't care who was targeting Hannah; he just wanted them stopped.

"Hello?" Ellen asked as she opened the door. "May I help you?"

"I'm Special Agent Drake, and this is my partner, Special Agent Luckman. We need to ask you a few questions."

"Is this about the robbery at Hannah's store?"

"It is," he confirmed.

"I don't know what I can tell you that Hannah or Vince couldn't, but sure, come on in."

She held the door farther open and led them into a living room filled with art supplies. There were half-finished canvases, a paint-stained easel, tables covered in paints, and brushes and pencils. Ellen was an artist, and although she had inherited her husband's businesses upon his death, Hannah had told them that she had hired someone to manage them for her because she wasn't a businesswoman.

"Vince said that the people who held him and Hannah and Jeff at gunpoint weren't the same people who had robbed the other jewelry stores," Ellen said as she shoved aside a stack of unused canvases from the couch and indicated they should sit.

"That's correct," Chloe replied.

"Did Vincent tell you anything else about the robbery?" Tom asked. It would be helpful to get his take on things.

"He didn't talk about it much. It's been a rough year for him. Losing his dad and his twin brother in such a way. Being in the car with them. My husband was killed instantly, but Charles was still alive. Vincent held his hand while he died. Then only seven months later, he's held at gunpoint. He didn't really want to talk about it. I was just so grateful he wasn't killed. I couldn't take losing him, too." Ellen plucked a tissue from the box on the table beside the armchair she had sunk down into and blotted at her wet eyes.

"Vincent dropped out of college?" Chloe asked. It made sense if Charles was pretending to be his brother. Vincent was the academic one and Charles would most likely have struggled to keep up in the pre-med classes, plus the accident was the perfect excuse to drop out and have no one question it. On the other hand, it could also be perfectly true. The traumatic loss of his brother and father could be a reason for the real Vincent to drop out of school.

"He didn't drop out," Ellen corrected. "He just took some time. He needed to be home as we both deal with the loss."

"Is he living here?" Tom asked.

"No, he has his own apartment, but it's nice to have him close by. I need him right now. I'm just so grateful that the cops turned up when they did. Those men had already shot Jeff; they would have shot Hannah and Vincent, too."

He understood timing.

If the timing hadn't worked out as it had, then he and Hannah would have been killed the night of the home invasion.

They had been saved by a nosy neighbor who noticed that their back door was open and that there were a mess of muddy footprints all over their back deck.

Thank goodness it had been raining for a week straight.

The elderly woman who lived behind them and spent all of her time watching the goings on in the neighborhood had known that he was an FBI agent and that there was no way he would leave his back door wide open. She had called 911, and the cops had arrived promptly.

Tom had been sure that he and Hannah didn't have long left when two cops had suddenly burst into the room.

The officers had ordered the six men, who had tortured him and Hannah for almost seven hours to put down their weapons and get down on the floor, but they had refused to comply. Four had been shot. Three died instantly. One was left in critical condition and later passed away. Two had followed the cops' directions.

The nosy neighbor had saved their lives; he could never thank her enough.

"Was it your idea or Vincent's to go and work for Hannah?" he asked.

"It was mine. I knew she needed someone on short notice, and Vincent was kind of at loose ends. I thought it would be good for him."

"How did he get along with Hannah?"

"He liked her, thought she was a fair boss."

"Does Vincent have a girlfriend?"

"No, he had been dating someone at college, but they broke up after the accident. It really shook up his whole world."

The accident was potentially the catalyst for all of this. It was time to confront Ellen with their suspicions and see how she reacted. Tom looked to Chloe and nodded. This was her theory, and she should be the one to ask the question.

"Mrs. Zimmerman, is Vincent really Charles?"

Ellen's face drained of all color.

Her mouth dropped open.

Her eyes scanned the room, seeking an escape route.

But there was none.

"Mrs. Zimmerman?" Chloe prompted.

"Wh—why would you a—ask me that?" she stammered.

"Is it true?" Tom asked quietly.

"Charles died," Ellen whispered.

"But did he die in the accident or did he die when he assumed his brother's identity?" Chloe pushed.

Ellen looked like a deer caught in the headlights. She didn't want to answer their questions, but she couldn't find another option. There was no way out. They already knew the answer. It was written all over her face.

Vincent Zimmerman had died in that car, and his brother Charles had decided to take over his identity.

"I couldn't lose him, too," Ellen whispered.

"It's true?" Tom asked. He wanted her to admit it out loud.

She nodded. "Yes. They would have taken him away from me."

"It was your idea?" Chloe asked.

She nodded again. "He was in shock when I got to the hospital. He hadn't spoken to anyone. He was still drinking so much, it was only a matter of time before they threw him in prison. I couldn't lose him, too. I told him if he pretended to be Vincent, then all the charges against him would just disappear. He could have a fresh start. He promised me," her eyes bored into them, begging them to believe her. "He promised me he wouldn't drink anymore."

An alcoholic couldn't make that kind of promise. But Hannah *had* said that she had never seen him drink. Maybe the shock of the accident and losing his brother and his father in one swoop had been enough to get him to quit cold turkey. They now knew that Chloe's theory had been correct, but that didn't mean that it was Charles who had set up the robbery.

"We think the robbery was an inside job," Tom told Ellen. "A ring was stolen after the robbery, after Hannah had given the code to Jeff and Charles. Someone came back and attacked Hannah a second time and then broke into her home and left her gifts."

"You think it's Charles?" Ellen looked genuinely shocked.

"Do you?"

"He's never said anything to me about Hannah before. I mean, nothing much. I didn't think he was interested in her or angry at her or anything."

"Have you seen him drink since the accident?" Charles was violent when he drank. If he wasn't sober, then they needed to be extra careful when they approached him.

"I—I'm not sure," Ellen admitted. Then her eyes grew wide; something had occurred to her.

"What?" he asked.

"Sometimes he spends the night here."

That didn't seem significant. "And?"

"When Charles stays here, he doesn't sleep in his old room, he stays in Vincent's."

Tom still didn't get it. "Why is that important?"

"Vincent's room looks straight into Hannah's."

Now he got it. Hannah liked to sleep with her curtains open so the moonlight could stream through into the room. She had always liked that. When they had first gotten married, it disturbed his sleep because he was used to complete dark when he slept, not half-light. If Hannah's blinds were open and Charles was sleeping in his brother's room that overlooked Hannah's, then it meant he could watch her while she slept.

～

1:31 P.M.

It was time.

They were here at the place Charles Zimmerman rented.

All they had to do was arrest him, then this was over, and Tom could go and give the good news to Hannah. With Charles in custody and Hannah safe, there was nothing left standing between them. They could finally sit down and work on their issues, or at least come up with a plan on how to get back what they'd lost.

Tom just prayed this went smoothly, that Charles didn't do anything stupid. But Charles was an alcoholic, and despite his promises to his mother that if he took over his brother's identity he would stop drinking, it didn't look like he'd been able to do it. If he'd been drinking already today, then he would be volatile and violent, which made for a potentially deadly combination.

"Ready to go in?" he asked his partner.

Chloe nodded. "Ready."

They had decided it would be best if only he and Chloe went in to talk to Charles. He already knew them from when they had interviewed him about the robbery. There were other cops here, waiting outside, ready to move in if things escalated, but Tom was hoping that wouldn't be necessary. Hopefully, Charles was ready to accept the consequences of his actions instead of trying to hide from them.

"Let's go," he said to Chloe. He was ready to end this.

Together, they headed to the eighth floor of the apartment building where Charles lived. The place was quiet. Thankfully, most people seemed to be out, braving the cold and snow on this the second last day before Christmas. Should Charles decide he wasn't going to go down without a fight, it was a good thing there wasn't going to be people about who might get caught in the crossfire.

Tom honestly didn't think Charles would try anything. But the teenager did have a history of pulling a gun on his family when drunk, and if he was backed into a corner, then there was no telling what he might try in a desperate bid for escape. Cops had cleared all the apartments on the eighth floor just to be safe.

Reaching Charles' front door, he knocked once.

There was no answer.

He knocked again, but didn't identify himself. He thought it was better to wait until Charles opened the door to do that.

Still, there was no answer.

They knew he was in there. One of the residents had confirmed that Charles had arrived home about an hour ago with a paper bag full of groceries and several rolls of Christmas wrapping paper and hadn't left. Maybe he had seen them and was hoping they thought he wasn't in there, or perhaps, his mother had managed to get word to him that they knew who he really was and were coming to get him.

He would give it one last try before they entered by force.

Tom knocked again, but still Charles refused to acknowledge them.

With a nod at Chloe, they both pulled out their weapons and he reached for the doorknob. It was unlocked and turned, and he opened the door. They were met with a long narrow hallway. There was a door to their left, another to their right, another farther down the hall on the right, and one at the end.

Taking the door on the left, Tom eased it open, and with Chloe covering him, he entered the room. It was a medium-sized kitchen, living, dining room. It was messy and looked just like he would expect a young, single, bachelor's home to look. There were empty food wrappers and bottles of soda and pizza boxes strewn everywhere. There were clothes piled on the sofa but Tom couldn't tell if they were clean or dirty. On a coffee table were a pair of scissors, the rolls of wrapping paper, and a couple of boxes. It looked like Charles had been doing his Christmas wrapping when they arrived.

There was no sign of Charles.

With the room cleared, they returned to the hallway and moved on to the first door on the right. It opened onto a small bedroom, clearly not the one Charles occupied because the only contents were a home gym and more litter piled about.

Again, there was no sign of Charles.

They moved on to the next door on the right. It was the bathroom. Surprisingly, this room was virtually spotless. The white tiles sparkled, the towels were hung neatly on a metal bar next to the bath, and the shower curtain was green and blue striped and looked nearly new. On the counter top, there was a toothbrush in a holder shaped like a snowman—that looked like something his mom would have picked out for him—a shaver, some deodorant, and aftershave. Charles was messy but obviously liked a clean bathroom.

He wasn't in there, either, which meant there was only one other room he could be in.

Cautiously, they approached the door at the end of the hall.

Tom swung the door slowly open and saw Charles Zimmerman sitting on the bed, a gun in his hands.

The weapon wasn't pointed at them, and Charles didn't look up at the opening door. Instead, he stared at the gun he clutched tightly in his hands.

"Charles," Tom said. "It's Special Agent Drake. We met after the robbery."

The teenager didn't look up.

Nor did he protest that his name was Vincent; it seemed like he had given up the charade.

"Put the gun down, Charles."

"It was my fault," the young man mumbled.

Was he admitting that he was the one who was after Hannah? "What was, Charles?" Tom asked, edging closer.

"The accident." He finally looked up, his dark eyes bottomless pools of pain and guilt.

"The car accident?" Tom asked, continuing to carefully maneuver himself closer to the bed. Charles still held the gun, and although he didn't appear to be intoxicated, as long as he held a weapon, he was a threat to himself and to them.

"We were arguing. *I* was arguing. I gave him the heart attack. He was trying to help me, but I didn't want to be helped. I wanted him to stop comparing me to Vincent. He was the good twin, I was the bad one. I accepted that. I just wanted them to leave me alone. But they wouldn't. I said some things I shouldn't, and he had a heart attack."

Tom doubted that Charles was the cause of his father's fatal heart attack, but he didn't think reasoning with the teenager would be productive right now. "Put the gun down, Charles. Your mother doesn't want to lose you, too."

"She'll be better off without me." Charles lifted the gun and pointed it at his own head.

"She loves you," he countered. "You're all she has left."

"When she finds out all the bad things I've done, that I was the reason she lost her husband and son, she won't want anything to do with me."

"She loves you," Tom repeated.

"No," Charles spat the word out. "She loved *Vincent*. She wished it was me who died. I wasn't the son she wanted. She wanted me to pretend that I was Vincent, that it was Charles who had died."

"Because she was afraid that you would go to prison and she would be all alone."

"Because she wanted Vincent more than me," Charles countered, he was growing increasingly agitated. "It was all her fault. *She's* the reason I started drinking. 'Why can't you be more like Vincent,' she would always say to me. He was the good one, the smart one, the sporty one, the musical one, the funny one, the one everyone loved. I was nothing."

Tom was sure that wasn't true, but he understood what it was like to feel overshadowed by a sibling. He had heard similar things growing up about his oldest sister. He had never taken his parents comments too seriously or committed them to heart like Charles obviously had. "Your mother loves you, Charles. She loved both her sons. Don't make her lose you, too."

"I'm going to prison. She's already lost me." Charles' face went faraway, his eyes grew distant, and Tom knew they had already lost him.

"Chloe."

That was all he needed to say.

His partner fired a split second before Charles Zimmerman did.

Charles' shot went high and the bullet plowed into the ceiling.

Chloe's shot hit its target perfectly, connecting with Charles' shoulder and stopping him from killing himself.

Both he and Chloe ran toward the teenager. Chloe grabbed the gun, which Charles had dropped when she'd shot him and moved it from his reach, while Tom grabbed the pillow from the bed and held it firmly against Charles' bleeding shoulder.

"Why did you do that? I'm better off dead," Charles mumbled before his eyes drooped closed.

For what he'd done to Hannah, Tom almost agreed with him. Whatever psychological problems the teenager had, which had no doubt been made worse by his alcohol abuse, that didn't give him the right to stalk and hurt Hannah. But having Charles commit suicide wouldn't have helped Hannah recover. The pain and fear would still be there.

Footsteps sounded down the hall, and paramedics and cops poured into the room. Tom stood back, relinquishing care of Charles to the professionals.

It was over.

Hannah was safe.

And all his.

≈

6:44 P.M.

He hadn't been so excited in years. Tom couldn't wait to show Hannah what he'd brought for her.

"Tom," she beamed at him as she threw open the door and saw him standing on her front porch. Then she grew serious. "It's over?"

"It is."

"Vincent—I mean, Charles—you arrested him?"

"He's in the hospital, but he's been arrested, and he's handcuffed to the bed."

"He really tried to kill himself?" She looked both shocked and distressed at the prospect.

"He did. He's a messed up young man, but that's not an excuse for his behavior." He didn't want Hannah taking responsibility for Charles' actions.

"So, it's over? It's really over?"

It sounded more like a question, so he answered, "It is. You're safe now, baby."

She threw her arms around his neck and hugged him tightly, pressing her face into his neck. "Thank you."

Tom wrapped his arms around her and lifted her feet off the ground, holding her every bit as tightly as she held him. "You don't have to thank me. You know I would do anything for you."

"You coming in?" she asked as he set her back down.

"Yes, but I have something for you first."

"An early Christmas gift?" her eyes lit up.

"Sort of." He walked down the steps of the porch to Hannah's front yard and picked up what he'd got for her.

Pure joy filled her face when she saw what it was. "Oh, Tom, it's perfect." She clapped her hands with glee, and came running over to kiss his cheek.

"You didn't have one," he told her, ridiculously pleased that she was so excited.

"I haven't, not since the last Christmas we spent together. I just couldn't. Not without you; it just wasn't the same."

"I haven't either," he told her. "But this year is different."

"Because we're together again," she smiled. Then her smile grew wider. "Let's get it inside. I'll go grab the boxes from the attic."

I'll get them, was on the tip of his tongue, but he stopped himself. Hannah was making an effort to let him do things for her, so he had to do the same. He couldn't keep wanting to step in and take over doing everything. "I'll help," he told her.

"Okay," she readily agreed and darted off back inside.

Tom laughed, and hiked up the seven-foot Christmas tree to drag it indoors. By the time he stepped through the front door, Hannah was already clunking around up in the attic.

He knew that Hannah loved to have the tree in the front window, so he hauled it into the living room. When he had it set up, he headed upstairs to the attic where he found Hannah had stacked all the boxes marked "Christmas" at the top of the steps.

"I forgot there were so many." She giggled as she saw him.

"Because you buy new decorations every single year," he reminded her as he grabbed the closest box.

"Well, you always bought me more." She poked her tongue out at him.

He couldn't help but laugh again. Hannah's Christmassy enthusiasm was contagious. It took them five trips to bring down all the boxes. Hannah apparently knew exactly what each one contained because she went straight to one and opened it, removing a skirt to go around the bottom of the tree, along with a string of fairy lights.

"Lights first," she told him once he'd put the Christmas tree skirt on.

"I know, I remember the routine."

When Hannah was happy with the placement of the lights, they moved on to tinsel, pulling out long garlands of sparkly gold tinsel. Again, Hannah was very particular with the placement of it and it took several tries before she was happy with the spacing between the lights and tinsel.

"Oh, Tom, look."

He turned to see what Hannah had pulled out of a box.

"Remember when you got this for me?"

Of course, he did. It was the first Christmas they'd spent together back when they were dating. "I think you cried when you opened it." He smiled at the memory.

"I loved it; it was the perfect gift. Can you put it on the tree for me?" Hannah asked.

"Sure." He took the shiny gold star and set it on the top of the tree.

"Now we can lay out all the decorations on the table so we can decide what should go where," she said as she opened up another box. "Make sure to group everything together. Angels, then snowmen, then candy canes, then Santas, and reindeer, and then miscellaneous."

He knew the drill. Once they got everything laid out, Hannah got busy adding each decoration to the tree, humming and hawing about just where each one should go. She liked everything to be just right, shiny decorations interspaced with wooden ones interspaced with plastic ones.

Tom sat on the couch and just watched her. If it was possible, she'd grown even more beautiful over the last three years. Especially like this, when she was happy and relaxed. It made her eyes shine a most gorgeous shade of bluey green, and her auburn hair looked luscious and beautiful against the purple sweater she wore.

"There." Hannah hung the final ornament and stood back to admire her work. "What do you think?"

Tom couldn't take his eyes off her. She was so happy, and he'd missed seeing her like this. "Perfect."

Hannah rolled her eyes at him. "I meant the tree."

"It's pretty perfect, too." He grinned.

She laughed and came to sit beside him on the sofa. When he wrapped an arm around her shoulders, she leaned into him. "I missed having a Christmas tree. I didn't realize how much until just now."

"You really did a great job with it."

"Thanks." She snuggled closer and rested her head against his shoulder. "There's only one thing that could make this night even better."

"Cocoa." Basically every night from Halloween through Christmas Day, they would sit on the couch in the evenings and sip steaming cups of hot cocoa. "I'll go make us some."

"Thanks, Tom."

Leaving Hannah to fiddle a little with the tree decorations, which she always did, tweaking things a little and then a little more, until she was completely satisfied, he headed to the kitchen feeling pretty satisfied himself. This was all he needed in life—the woman he loved by his side. Everything else was just icing on the cake.

"Here you go, one mug of steaming hot cocoa coming right up," Tom announced as he carried the mugs back into the living room.

Hannah didn't answer. She was sitting on the sofa where he'd left her, but as he got closer, he saw tears were trickling down her cheeks. When he'd gone to the kitchen, she'd been so happy. Now, she was crying.

Quickly, he set the mugs on the table and went to her, "Baby, what's wrong?"

"What are we doing?"

Confused, he answered, "Decorating the Christmas tree."

"No, I mean with us." She met his gaze squarely, "Are we back together now?"

Fighting the urge to let Hannah confirm that first, he couldn't be a coward. "Yes. At least, as far as I'm concerned."

"We have a lot we need to talk about."

"We do," he agreed.

"You can't be trying to save me anymore. I don't need you to save me. I never did. All I needed was just for you to be there for me."

"I tried to be there for you, but you kept shutting me out."

"That wasn't intentional. I wasn't trying to shut you out. I was just trying to prove to myself and to you and to everyone else, that I wasn't a victim. That I wasn't helpless and I wasn't going to break."

"I never thought you would, Hannah. You are the single strongest person I know." He sat beside her and took her hands. How had he failed to let her know how amazing he thought she was?

"I didn't know you thought that. I thought you thought that I couldn't do anything on my own, that I needed you to save me."

"But I didn't. I didn't save you; instead, I got you hurt." His grip on her hands loosened, but she tightened hers, latching on to his fingers.

"No one but you blamed you for what happened. There were six men, Tom. *Six* men. Six men with *guns*. You were just one man. You're not a superhero and you don't have magical powers. There was nothing you could have done against six armed men. The odds were just stacked too firmly against you."

Logically, he knew Hannah was right, but she was his wife, and he was an FBI agent. He should have been able to protect her, keep her safe. Instead, he'd failed her. Failed the one person he loved the most in the world.

Reading his expression, Hannah released his hands and twisted hers together in her lap. "I was so hurt when you turned your back on me. It felt like you abandoned me. I thought you were the one person that I could always count on to be there for me."

"You asked me before if I would have stayed if you had asked me to. I would have. I didn't want to walk away. I was hurt, too. I wanted to help you, but you wouldn't let me. I understand that you wanted to rebuild your confidence and your strength, but you shut me out every chance you got."

"You walked away because of your guilt," she corrected. "And I let you because I was afraid I couldn't be the wife you deserved anymore."

He reached out and cupped her face in his hand, his thumb wiped away her still-falling tears. "You have *always* been the wife I wanted. We were both hurting, and we made it worse by shutting each other out."

"We can't do that this time. We have to communicate, we have to compromise, we have to support each other and try to see things from the other person's point of view."

"I will work on being your husband and not your bodyguard. I'll give you space when you need it and not try to do everything for you, so you know how strong I think you are."

"And I'll work on reminding myself that letting you help me isn't a bad thing. That I can be strong and still accept help, that the two aren't mutually exclusive. And I will remind you every day that what happened was not your fault, so that maybe one day you'll believe it."

"Deal," he held out his hand.

"Deal," Hannah took it and shook it.

They'd just taken the first—and biggest—step in repairing their relationship and getting back what they had lost.

~

10:52 P.M.

This had been the most perfect day.

She felt so happy, so light, so free. Hannah hadn't felt this way since the day before the home invasion.

She scrambled up onto her knees and took Tom's face in her hands, kissing him. The kind of kiss that held everything that went with three long years of separation.

Tom kissed her back, one of his hands curling around her neck, his fingers threading through her hair. His other hand traced around the small of her back and landed on her hip, drawing her closer so she was right up against his body. Her hands dropped to his chest to brace herself as he deepened the kiss.

Too soon, he broke contact. He was panting, his eyes glittering with desire and self-restraint.

But she didn't want restraint.

She wanted Tom.

More than that, she *needed* him.

"Hannah."

That was all he said, but it was enough. He looked so conflicted. He wanted to take things further. She knew he did—she could feel the evidence of his desire. But he also wasn't sure if they were ready to take that step. If *she* was ready. They hadn't been intimate since she'd been raped.

At first, it had been too soon. She hadn't been able to even think about sex after what had happened. And she was pretty sure Tom had felt the same way. Then they had drifted apart. They'd barely been able to stand in the same room without bickering, let alone been close enough to make love.

After the divorce, she had just never met anyone she cared about enough to want to sleep with.

From the look on Tom's face, he was putting the ball in her court. If she wanted to continue, he would. If she said stop, he would do that, too.

But Hannah didn't want to stop.

She was ready to take this next step in her recovery.

There was a time when she hadn't been sure that she would ever reach this point. She had thought that the rape might have ruined sex for her forever. She'd spoken with her therapist about it, and Dr. Langley had told her that she would know if and when she was ready to take that step, and that however long it took her was fine. There was no timeline for recovering from what she had been through.

Right now, her body was telling her that she was ready.

"Let's go upstairs." She stood, grabbing Tom's hand on the way and tugging him to his feet.

"Are you sure?"

"Yes," she answered honestly.

"Have you . . .? Since . . .?" he asked awkwardly.

"No."

"Garry?"

"We never. I haven't slept with anyone else since we broke up. I couldn't. I didn't love them."

Tom looked relieved to hear that she and Garry hadn't had sex. She didn't need to ask him if he'd been intimate with any of the women he'd dated since their divorce. She could read in his face that he had. Just as she could read that it hadn't meant anything to him. Part of her wished that he hadn't, but another part—the bigger part—understood that it hadn't been about the women. It had been about him, proving to himself that what had happened hadn't affected him, that he wasn't a victim, too, and that his life could go on as though nothing had happened.

It wasn't true, of course.

But it was what he had needed to tell himself so he could survive.

This was what was important.

What was happening between them right now.

Tom picked her up and she wrapped her legs around his waist, kissing him as he carried her up the stairs and down the hall to her bedroom.

Inside, he laid her down on the bed, and knelt above her. "You're so beautiful," he said, his voice husky, as he brushed the back of his knuckles across her cheeks.

"You're pretty beautiful yourself," she said as her fingertips traced over every inch of his face as though seeing it for the first time.

His hands dropped to the buttons of her purple sweater, undoing them slowly. As her top opened, his face changed—growing fierce as he looked at the white gauze bandages covering the knife wounds on her chest. One of his big hands covered it, as though attempting to block it out.

"I'm sorry, Hannah. I hate that you got hurt." His eyes sparked with anger.

"I'm okay, Tom," she reminded him.

"You might not have been." The anger turned to raw fear. "If anything happened to you . . ." He trailed off and she felt his entire body shudder.

"I feel the same about you." Her fingers curled into his sweater and held on tightly.

She could feel tears welling in her eyes, and Tom must have noticed, too, because he leaned down and kissed her. "You are breathtaking," he murmured against her lips.

Hannah tensed at his words. She didn't feel beautiful right now, not with a ten-inch gash running from her cheek down her neck and onto her chest. She knew Tom didn't care about it, and she knew that over time the gash would heal and the scar would fade, but it would always be there, and people would know that someone had hurt her just by looking at her. That made her feel so exposed and vulnerable.

"I don't care about the cut." Tom read what she was feeling in her face. "I hate that Charles got you hurt, but it doesn't make you any less beautiful."

"It will leave a scar."

"It will."

"Everyone will know when they look at me that I'm a victim."

"Hannah," Tom said sternly, "when people look at you, they don't see a victim, they see a survivor. There's a difference. When I look at this cut, I see your strength—you fought back, and you amaze me." His lips touched her cheek beside the cut, then trailed a line of kisses along it. His hands undid her jeans and he slid them down her legs, leaving her mostly undressed and him still fully clothed.

"How come you still have all your clothes on? That seems unfair." She gave a nervous laugh. As much as she wanted to do this, she was a little anxious about how she would react. She wanted it to be like making love to Tom had always been, but what if the rape had changed things? What if she freaked out right in the middle of things? What if it triggered flashbacks? What if she couldn't do it? What if she could never do it again?

"I think we can rectify that," he smiled, pulling his sweater off.

She stared at the six-pack she remembered so well, and of their own volition, her hands lifted to touch him.

Tom took her hands one by one and slid her arms out of her sweater, and since she wasn't wearing a bra, that left her in only her panties. Then he kissed her again, while one of his hands tugged on the waistband of her underwear.

Hannah tensed. She didn't mean to; she just couldn't help it.

"Do you want to stop, sweetheart?" Tom asked, as he noticed the sudden change in her body language.

"No," she answered, and she really didn't. "It's just . . ."

"Your first time and you're a little nervous. We'll go slowly, and if you want to stop, then all you have to do is say so," he promised.

"I love you, Tom." Her whole body swelled with emotion. Love, gratitude, trust, faith; she loved Tom so much, and she wished she hadn't let what had happened rip them apart.

"I love you, too." His fingers stroked her hair, then trailed down her body with a feather soft touch that made her skin goose pimple, and she shivered with delight.

Then he was kissing her again, and his hand found its way inside her underwear, and all her fears and anxieties melted away.

She wasn't afraid anymore.

She was safe with Tom.

Because he loved her and she loved him and together they were stronger than they were on their own.

This day really was the most perfect day ever.

CHAPTER

Seven

December 24th
4:20 A.M.

She hadn't come to him.

It was starting to make him angry.

What else did he have to do to get her to notice him?

He had tried to scare her into coming running straight into his waiting arms. Twice. And he had left her gifts that laid his heart bare.

Yet still, nothing.

He had even allowed himself to be shot for her, and still, she didn't come to him.

Jeff Shields had had enough.

Hannah *was* going to be his.

Surely, he had proved his love to her already. She had to have seen what she meant to him. He stayed after work every single day to help her clean up so that she could get home a little earlier. He took on extra responsibilities to lighten her load a little. He filled in for her whenever she was sick. She paid him well, and extra for every additional thing he did to help her, but he didn't do it for the money. He did it for her. Because he loved to see her smile, and he loved her laugh even more, and he loved the gratitude that shone from her eyes whenever he did something for her.

He had thought that would be enough, that he did those things for her because he loved her.

For a while, he thought it might be working. Hannah didn't have a lot of friends. She mostly kept to herself, and her main focus was her business, which worked out perfectly for him. They spent so much time together, and he seemed to make her happy and relaxed. He thought she enjoyed his company. Jeff had even considered confessing his feelings to her and asking her out.

But Hannah kept rebuffing his attempts.

Whenever he hinted at the two of them possibly doing something outside of work, she always had an excuse. When she had been having her house repainted, he had offered to come and help. When she had taken a rare weekend away in the summer, he had offered to stop by her house and pick up her mail. When her car broke down and she had to take a taxi or the bus home and to the homeless shelter for her shift, he had offered to drive her.

All those times she had said no.

It was then that he had realized it wasn't because she didn't appreciate him or enjoy spending time with him. It was because she was so strong—so independent—that she just couldn't bring herself to accept help, from anyone. Even him.

That was when he had known for sure that she just needed a little push to make her realize that when she needed someone he would be there for her, and that she could accept help from him and still be her strong, independent self. The robbery had seemed like the perfect idea because of the string of robberies in the area. He'd thought if he took advantage of that, then everyone would just assume the one at Hannah's store was committed by the same people that committed the others. It might have worked, too, if he'd been able to find a third man to participate.

Allowing himself to get shot had been a scary prospect, but he'd thought it was a nice added touch. He knew Hannah had a phobia of guns, and that if the armed men demanded the code to the safe she wouldn't be able to give it to them. It had all run smoothly, like clockwork, and he had been able to come running in and be the hero who saved her from being hurt.

That act of heroism was supposed to send her right to him.

And it might have if that stupid ex-husband of hers hadn't come back into her life. How unlucky was he that of all the FBI agents in the country, the one who was working the robbery heists was Hannah's ex-husband?

The man was ruining everything.

He had chosen to toss Hannah away. He couldn't just waltz back into her life and try to take her back.

Hannah hadn't even mentioned the man in the years they had known each other, so he couldn't mean all that much to her.

Why did that man have to come back now?

Because of her ex, Hannah wasn't even thinking about him. She was too busy with the FBI agent to even come and visit him again.

She should be here.

With him.

It wasn't fair.

Didn't she get his gifts? Didn't she understand how much he loved her? Didn't she see what he was trying to say to her?

Maybe she didn't.

He had never just come right out and said that he loved her. And Hannah was scared to let people get too close to her because of what had happened to her. He was going to have to be more understanding. He was also going to have to be more transparent. If he loved Hannah, then he had to tell her. He couldn't just expect her to figure it out herself.

Which was exactly why he had come here.

Carefully, he opened Hannah's back door and snuck inside. When Jeff stepped into her kitchen, he immediately felt the familiar sense of peace wash over him. This was where he belonged—here with the woman he loved by his side.

Quietly, he tiptoed through the kitchen and dining room, heading for the stairs, intending to go up to Hannah's bedroom. But in the hall, he paused. There was a Christmas tree in her living room.

That could mean only one thing.

Special Agent Tom Drake had been here.

Or maybe he still was. He could be upstairs sharing Hannah's bed.

Rage flashed through him, like he had been struck by lightning. He balled his hands into fists and screamed a silent scream. He didn't want that man anywhere near his Hannah. Just because he was an FBI agent, he thought he was so much better than everyone else. Jeff hadn't liked him from the moment the man and his partner had walked into his hospital room to interview him about the robbery.

He hated him.

Hated him.

He wanted to grab the man and rip him to shreds with his bare hands. He didn't care that he was fifty-four and Tom Drake was only thirty. Fury would strengthen him; righteousness was on his side.

He wanted what was best for Hannah. Tom Drake only cared about himself. He had obviously brought a Christmas tree here to try and trick Hannah. To squirm his way into her good graces. Tom had probably pressured Hannah into going to bed with him.

It was unacceptable.

Jeff would not allow Tom to hurt Hannah all over again.

He had to save her, protect her, declare his undying love for her.

He was going to make Hannah understand.

Whatever it took.

She loved Christmas. Even though she tried to hide it, he knew. So, this seemed like the perfect time to sit her down and explain to her how much she meant to him and how everything that he had done was for her.

All he had to do was get rid of Tom Drake first. Killing him might not be smart, although it would certainly be satisfying. The man was a Special Agent in the FBI, and they were bound to want to hunt down whoever had killed one of their own.

In the end, Jeff really didn't care about the man. He just wanted him away from Hannah. Far away.

Maybe the safer option would be to wait here for Hannah to be alone, then to take her someplace where it was just the two of them. Where he could tell her everything without fear of being interrupted or of anyone trying to get between them.

Yes.

That was what he would do.

Soon.

Soon he would have her.

She would understand.

She would.

She had to.

He would rather die than not have Hannah for his very own.

~

6:41 A.M.

Hannah woke slowly.

The first thing to cross her consciousness was the arms that she was wrapped up in.

Although Tom was still fast asleep, his grip on her wasn't loose. It was like even in sleep he took protecting her seriously.

Something had changed yesterday. She no longer resented his protective streak. She no longer took it as an indication that he thought she was weak and helpless and fragile. Now she knew he didn't see her as a victim, but as a survivor. Knowing that made accepting his need to protect her and keep her safe so much easier.

Last night had been so amazing. Tom knew her body so well. He knew just where to touch her and how to drive her wild. She needn't have worried about freaking out, or being unable to perform, or having flashbacks. Once she and Tom started, it became all about the two of them. The home invasion and the rape had been the farthest things from her mind.

As amazing as last night was, this was better.

Waking up in her bed, having spent the entire night in it without a single nightmare, with Tom's warm body at her side was the best way to wake up. She had draped herself over him while they'd been asleep. When they'd finished their lovemaking and laid down, she had been spooned against Tom with her back to his front and his arm locked around her waist. But now, he was on his back and her head was on his chest, her leg hooked around his. His breath tickled her forehead as it whooshed in and out, and the thump of his heart beneath her ear had apparently been the reassurance her brain needed to let go of the nightmares.

She could get used to this.

Her stomach rumbled. She and Tom had been so busy last night decorating the tree that she hadn't eaten any dinner. She should go and make Tom breakfast. He loved her Belgium waffles as much as she loved his French toast.

As carefully as she could, so as not to disturb him, Hannah slid out from underneath Tom's arm and climbed out of her huge, king-size sleigh bed. Their clothes were strewn on the floor around the bed, lying right where they had tossed them last night. Although they were in her bedroom and her closet was right here, Hannah picked up Tom's discarded shirt and shrugged into it. She loved wearing Tom's clothes around the house. It had always made her feel closer to him.

The hardwood floors were cold beneath her bare feet as she crept out of the bedroom and down the hall. Usually she wore socks around the house in the wintertime because her feet always got cold, but she had forgotten to grab a pair. Oh well, once she got busy she wouldn't notice the cold so much.

In the hall, she stopped.

The Christmas tree was breathtaking.

She couldn't take her eyes off it.

She had been so surprised when Tom brought it over, she hadn't even been thinking about decorating for Christmas, but she was so glad he had thought of it. He could be so thoughtful sometimes. Well, most of the time, really.

It had felt just like old times. Her obsessing over the placement of each decoration, Tom watching her and then patiently moving them from place to place on the tree until she was happy with the result.

She wanted that again.

She and Tom had been so happy together, and now they had a chance to have that back. To let go of the pain of the last three years and rebuild their lives. Maybe one day they'd even have a family of their own, and their kids would be right there beside them, excitedly decorating the house and waiting for Santa Claus to come. Hannah couldn't help but smile at the thought. She couldn't wait to have Tom's baby growing inside of her. Once things had settled between them, then they could start trying, but not until then. Hannah didn't want to bring a baby into the picture until things between Tom and her were stable.

Maybe they should decorate the rest of the house today. There was the wreath for the front door and garlands for the banisters and more fairy lights than any home needed. There was the Christmas village with shops and houses and Santa's village. Plus, there was an assortment of various figurines and other decorations. She had so many things that every available spare inch of space was covered with them.

And her snow globe collection.

She'd been obsessed with them ever since she could remember, and every single year, her parents had given her one as a Christmas gift. At her and Tom's old house, she had set them all out along the fireplace mantles in the living room, dining room, and master bedroom. She could do that here, too. Her house had four fireplaces. In her mind, fireplaces went with Christmas, so she always lived in a house that had at least one of them.

With a big grin on her face, she rolled up her sleeves and was about to turn around to head to the kitchen and get started on breakfast when someone suddenly grabbed her from behind.

For a moment, her mind tried to convince her that it was just Tom.

But he would have announced himself. Or, if he was trying to surprise her, he would have lifted her off her feet and swung her up into the air.

This wasn't Tom.

He felt different.

He smelled different.

"Hannah."

The voice.

She knew who it was.

It was Jeff Shields.

It wasn't Vincent who had been stalking her, who had set up the robbery, and broken in here to leave her gifts. It was Jeff.

And he'd come back.

"Don't make a sound. You call him and I'll shoot him on the spot," his voice spoke in her ear.

She believed him.

Completely.

Because his voice wasn't angry, it wasn't agitated, it wasn't anxious. It was absolutely, perfectly calm.

She had to stay composed. Tom was right upstairs. He was bound to come down here sooner or later; she just had to hold it together until then.

Something cold touched her temple, right over the bruise she'd received the night of the robbery.

Jeff had a gun.

A gun.

She almost fainted on the spot.

Deciding to work on her phobia was one thing. Knowing that her ex-husband who would never lay a hand on her had his weapon holstered at his side was one thing. But knowing that someone who meant her harm, who had gotten her hurt twice already, was holding a gun to her head was more than she could bear.

No.

She had to bear it.

She couldn't give up. She couldn't let him kill her because that would kill Tom.

"Wh-what do you w-want, J-Jeff?"

"You. I want you. I love you, Hannah."

He didn't love her. If he loved her, he would never hurt her. He was obsessed with her. That was a completely different thing. A terrifying thing.

"Th-then let me go. Please. You know I hate guns."

"I don't want to hurt you, Hannah. I just need to make sure you understand. I love you. I *love* you so much."

One of his hands held the gun to her temple, and the other he had on her shoulder, keeping her pinned against his chest. But he let it drop down to the hem of her shirt—beneath which she was completely naked —and slowly lifted it.

His hand splayed on her stomach. Hannah wanted to squirm away from him, but she was afraid to move. There was a chance she could talk her way out of this, but not if she made him angry.

"You're so beautiful." His hot breath was repugnant against her ear. When Tom called her beautiful, it made her feel like a goddess. When Jeff said it, it made her want to curl up in a ball and die.

His hand moved up her stomach to cover her breast. His hand was rough against her skin, and he squeezed her injured breast, making her suck in a pained breath.

"I can make you happy. So happy. If only you'd let me."

He was insane.

Jeff really and truly thought not only that he loved her but that she could love him back.

His hand left her breast, and she let out a sigh of relief.

Her relief wasn't long lived.

His hand didn't leave her body.

Instead, it dipped between her legs.

She couldn't go through this again.

She couldn't.

Her entire body clenched and she whimpered.

Her mews of distress must have upset Jeff, because he withdrew his hand. "I love you, Hannah. If you just give me a chance, I can show you. I can make you happy. I want to make you happy, and I want to be with you, always. Forever."

7:11 A.M.

Tom was cold.

The feeling ripped him out of sleep.

Hannah was gone.

He rolled over and stretched, the kind of long contented stretch that a cat gave. Last night had been amazing. He knew Hannah had been afraid that she couldn't cope with sex after her assault, but once she let go of that fear, it had been just like old times.

Then afterward, they had fallen asleep in each other's arms. Hannah had slept peacefully through the night. When he'd awakened at six, hot, he'd found her draped across him. The feel of her body lying on his was something he could never get enough of, and being completely content, he had gone straight back to sleep.

Hannah must have woken up shortly after and decided to get up. If he knew her, and he did, she probably went to make breakfast. Maybe once they'd had breakfast he could convince her to come back to bed with him, although knowing Hannah, she was probably going to want to finish decorating the house for Christmas. He couldn't help but smile, and he couldn't wait to celebrate another Christmas with her.

She must have put on his shirt, because it wasn't on the floor where he'd tossed it last night. For some reason, she liked wearing his clothes around the house. Pulling on his pants, he padded down the hall, anxious to find Hannah. He didn't like not having her in his line of sight. The last few days had taken a toll on both of them, and it would take them both a while to recover.

At the top of the steps, he froze.

Jeff Shields was standing in the hall, holding a gun to Hannah's head.

His anger flared at the sight of the woman he loved in danger once again, but he took his anger and stowed it, it wasn't going to be productive right now.

Yesterday, he'd put his gun in one of Hannah's spare bedrooms. He hadn't wanted the sight of it to upset her, but he'd wanted to keep it close by. Why? He hadn't been sure. Intuition, maybe. Whatever the reason, he didn't have time to analyze it.

Grabbing his weapon, he placed a quick call to Chloe. His partner answered on the second ring. "Hostage situation at Hannah's house. It wasn't Charles Zimmerman; it was Jeff Shields. He has a gun on Hannah."

Not bothering to waste time listening to Chloe's reply, he hung up and headed back to the stairs. Jeff and Hannah's backs were toward him, so they didn't see him quietly make his way down the steps.

Jeff was whispering in Hannah's ear. "I love you, Hannah. If you just give me a chance, I can show you. I can make you happy, and I want to make you happy. I want to be with you, always. Forever."

"Let her go, Jeff," Tom said.

The older man spun around, bringing Hannah with him, his gun never dipping from where it was shoved against her temple.

Hannah's eyes met his, panicked and full of fear, but also full of trust. She believed that he would get her out of this alive.

He prayed her trust was well-founded.

"I love her." Jeff's brown eyes were fierce.

"Then let her go; you know she's afraid of guns."

"Because of *you*," the man spat. The arm he held across Hannah's chest tightened, and her eyes bulged as it pressed against her neck, hampering her ability to breathe. "You let her get hurt. Then you just threw her away. I want to take care of her. I want to make her happy. I want her to know that I love her."

He kept his gaze fixed firmly on Jeff. If he looked at Hannah, saw the fear on her face, he would feed off that fear, and that would prevent him from doing his job. "I love Hannah, too. I don't want to see her hurt or scared."

"You don't love her," Jeff growled. "You. Don't. Love. Her."

Hannah cried out as he ground the gun into her temple. She was forced to stand on her tippy-toes, her hands clawing at Jeff's arm, so she could breathe. She was shaking; he guessed from a mixture of cold and shock.

"You lost someone," Tom went with his hunch because it was the only thing he could think of to keep Jeff talking until help arrived.

Jeff froze.

Shock filled his face.

The gun wavered for a moment, and Tom thought he was going to lower it, but then Jeff rammed it into Hannah's head, making her cry out again. "How did you know that?" Jeff demanded.

"Who was she?" He'd started down this road, and he had no choice but to follow it through and continue to trust his gut.

"She is none of your business."

"You cared about her. You loved her. You want to save Hannah because you love her, too. Hannah reminds you of her. Did someone hurt her?"

"I'm not talking about her. I'm here for Hannah. You didn't want her. You threw her away, but I was there. I helped her. I supported her. When she needed someone, I was there."

"And I'm sure she appreciated it. I'm sure it meant a lot to her to have someone like you in her life."

"If *you* hadn't come back, she would have been mine. You ruined everything."

Tom was starting to wonder if Jeff's end game was killing him and then abducting Hannah, taking her someplace and trying to make her reciprocate his feelings. When that didn't happen, Jeff would kill Hannah, too. He prayed help arrived soon. He was going to have to push harder and hope that he didn't go too far. "Was she raped, Jeff? The woman you loved?"

Jeff began to vibrate with emotion. His eyes grew moist. "Penny."

"Did someone hurt Penny?" He gentled his voice. Jeff already didn't like him, and he didn't want to give the older man another reason to shoot him.

"She was walking home from school. He grabbed her. Dragged her into an alley. Assaulted her."

"How old was she?"

"Sixteen. Only sixteen."

"She was your girlfriend?"

Jeff nodded.

"What happened to her?"

"Suicide," the man mumbled.

He would never have thought that an-almost-four-decade-old crime could have had such long lasting and far reaching consequences. "I'm sorry."

It didn't appear that Jeff heard him. The older man was lost in thought. "I walked away from her. I turned my back on her. I was sixteen and scared. I didn't know how to help a girl deal with rape. I was just a kid. I didn't know what to say. I didn't know what to do. She would cry. She was so lost. I broke up with her. When she needed someone the most, I wasn't there. She overdosed on her anti-depressants a month after I dumped her."

"Penny's suicide wasn't your fault, Jeff. Trauma like that messes with your head. It makes you see things—the world and yourself— differently."

"Not Hannah," Jeff protested. "She survived. Her assault made her grow stronger."

Tom couldn't argue with that. Hannah was amazing. Jeff had taken his misplaced guilt over his teenage girlfriend's suicide and put it on Hannah. She was what he believed that Penny should have been— strong and independent, accepting what had happened and working on overcoming it. He had both admired Hannah's strength but also seen it as an obstacle to overcome in getting to her. He had needed to break Hannah to get her to come to him. Only that would never happen. Hannah was unbreakable. She would never love Jeff. She would never give him what he wanted.

"I wasn't there for Penny, but I've been here for Hannah. I've admired her strength, and I want to make her stronger by loving her. I would never throw her away like you did. I won't ever turn my back on her. I won't ever let her go."

Tom believed that.

He was going to have to make his move, or this was not going to end well. Although he wanted to wait for Chloe and backup to arrive, he didn't think he was going to have that much time. He wasn't a trained hostage negotiator, but he knew the basics—active listening, empathy, rapport, influence, change behavior. He just didn't think they were going to work in this situation. In Jeff's mind, Tom was the problem. He was the obstacle to getting what he wanted; it was personal. Jeff hated him for hurting Hannah by walking away and for coming back into her life and getting between him and Hannah.

Hannah was still on her tippy-toes and her legs were beginning to tremble from being forced to remain in that position, but if she didn't, then Jeff's arm would be crushing her throat and preventing her from breathing. She was wearing out. Right now, Jeff's attention was focused on him, but when Hannah's legs gave out, she would draw his attention back to her. Tom wanted to keep Jeff's focus. As long as he did, Hannah was marginally safer. If he could get Jeff angry enough to fire a shot at him, then Hannah could get free and get to safety.

"I believe that you love Hannah, Jeff. I believe that everything that you've done is because you wanted to show her just how much you loved her. But this isn't the way. Scaring her and paying people to hurt her doesn't show her your love. When you love someone, you have to set aside your own needs and wants and desires to do what's best for them. And what's best for Hannah right now is for you to let her go. She understands that you love her. You don't need to hold a gun to her head and scare her anymore. Let her go. Show her how much you love her. Show her that you want to put her before yourself."

~

7:29 A.M.

"Are you questioning my love for Hannah?" Jeff's anger exploded.

His grip on her tightened once again, and he ground his gun harder into her temple. Hannah tried not to cry out because she knew it would distract Tom, and she didn't want to do that. Her life was in his hands, and she trusted him to get her out of this alive.

She was trying to do her part. She kept herself balanced on her tiptoes, but her legs were beginning to shake. She was using her grip on Jeff's forearm to help steady herself. She was shivering, and cold air was seeping up under the shirt she wore, curling around her naked flesh and reminding her of the feel of Jeff's hand on her skin. At least he hadn't done anything more than touch her breast and move his hand between her legs. When he'd realized he was upsetting her, he'd stopped before he put anything inside her.

Her mind wanted to keep throwing her back into the past, but this wasn't three years ago. She and Tom weren't helpless at the hands of six evil men who had come to their home with the sole purpose of torturing and killing them.

This was Jeff.

And whether she had seen who he truly was or not, she knew him.

Right now, Tom was making him so angry. Pushing him by making him recount the story of his teenage girlfriend who had been raped and committed suicide. Hannah had had no idea that Jeff had been through that. She wished he'd told her. She might have been able to give him some insight into some of the things that might have been going through Penny's head. Particularly, since Jeff had broken up with Penny shortly following her assault, and she and Tom had gotten divorced shortly after hers. That was obviously the reason he had developed this obsession with her.

She was afraid that if Tom kept antagonizing Jeff, then Jeff was going to shoot him. She was even more afraid that that was exactly what Tom was hoping would happen. That if he kept Jeff's focus and got him angry enough to fire off a shot at him then the gun would no longer be at her head, and she might be able to get away.

But she had no intention of letting that happen. She didn't want Tom to sacrifice himself for her, and she didn't want to risk him being hurt. He had had time to get his gun, so she assumed that he had also called for help, but they had no idea when that help would arrive, and Jeff was growing more agitated by the second.

The two men continued to talk, but she had tuned out their words. All her energy was focused on keeping herself balanced and trying to figure out a way where all three of them walked out of this alive. And if that couldn't happen, then at least she and Tom walked out of this alive. She didn't want Jeff to die, but she had obviously never really known him, and he wasn't the man that she thought he was. If killing him was the only way she and Tom survived, then she would be okay with that.

Tom obviously said something that angered Jeff again because he squeezed her so tightly she couldn't stop an agonized cry from escaping her lips. The gun was pressed so tightly against her head that she could feel it cutting into her flesh. A small trickle of blood dribbled down her face.

Blood.

That gave her an idea.

Jeff was injured. He had gotten himself shot in the robbery, and she assumed it was because he wanted her to see him as the hero who came running in to save her when the robbers threatened to shoot her. From the way he squeezed her, the wound didn't appear to be giving him too much trouble but it still had to be causing him pain.

Maybe she could take advantage of that.

If she waited until the gun dropped a little, then she could gouge her hand into the wound, which might be enough to make him let her go. Her hands were already wrapped around his left arm, using it for leverage to keep enough space between it and her neck so that she could breathe. His right hand held the gun at her head, and the distance between her hands and his injured right shoulder wasn't far. She thought she could make it.

It would be risky, though.

If she mistimed it, he could shoot her.

Kill her.

But she was going to have to take that risk. What other choices did she have? She could do nothing and let Jeff shoot both her and Tom. Or just Tom. And she was pretty sure that if Jeff killed or seriously wounded Tom, he would drag her out of here and away somewhere where he thought he could keep her and make her fall in love with him. That was never going to happen, and sooner or later Jeff would realize that and kill her, too.

She had to do this.

It might be the only way. Hannah didn't think that Tom could talk Jeff into releasing them and giving himself up.

"Cops are going to be here any minute, Jeff," Tom was saying. "You made a mistake with Penny by putting your needs ahead of hers. Don't make the same mistake with Hannah."

"Everything I've done has been for her," Jeff screamed in her ear. "I tried to help her, to make her see that having someone there for her wasn't a bad thing. It's you. You failed her. I saved her."

"You hurt her. You're hurting her right now. Don't make this worse, Jeff. Please. If you love Hannah as much as you say you do, then let her go. Do the right thing, prove that love."

"Prove my love? I've proved it over and over and over again," Jeff raged. As he spoke, the gun moved away from her head. Not a lot, but it was no longer pressed against her temple.

This was it.

It was now or never.

She might not get another chance.

She had to make her move.

She was only going to have one shot at this.

If she missed her target, then both she and Tom could wind up dead.

Before she could overthink things and talk herself out of it, Hannah darted her hand toward Jeff's wound. She connected and dug her fingers in.

Jeff howled and released her.

She spun out of his grip.

He whirled on her.

His gun was pointed directly at her.

His brown eyes, which at one time she had considered to be those of a friend she trusted and cared about, were now wild with fury and doused in obsession.

He would rather kill her than let her go.

Hannah could see it in his face.

He was going to fire.

She could see it in his eyes.

Hannah braced herself for the onslaught of pain that would come when the bullet hit her.

She readied herself to die.

Mentally, she said her goodbyes to Tom and thanked him for giving her one last joyful, special, magical night.

The gun went off.

The sound seemed amplified inside her head.

Blood splattered everywhere.

Jeff fell.

Tom grabbed her hand, yanking her hard up against his chest.

Keeping her close, he kicked Jeff's gun away from him.

It took Hannah's brain a moment to process what had happened.

Jeff hadn't shot her; Tom had shot Jeff.

She had been right beside Jeff when Tom shot him. She had his blood and brains all over her.

She started to shake in earnest as it began to sink in just how close she and Tom had come to dying.

Tom yelled something, but the words didn't penetrate the haze that was settling on her.

The room descended into chaos as people flooded in.

Cops, she supposed.

Hannah didn't care who was here; all she cared about was that they were alive. She pressed herself closer to Tom and clung to him. What would she have done if anything had happened to him?

"Shh. It's all right, baby, it's over now. You're safe, sweetheart. You're safe." Tom was stroking her hair, and she suddenly remembered that she was covered in Jeff's blood.

"I'm sorry, I'm getting it all over you." She tried to step out of Tom's embrace.

He tightened his hold on her, pulling her closer, cocooning her in safety and warmth. Not just warmth that heated her cold body, but warmth that seeped down inside her, heating her heart that had been so badly damaged by everything that had happened three years ago.

"Thank you," she whispered against his chest. "You saved my life."

"Actually, I think you saved yourself," Tom said. "And me."

"I think we saved each other," she said.

"We're a pretty good team."

"We are," she agreed. "But maybe no more talk about saving."

"Agreed." He gently eased her off his chest and held her at arm's length, "Now let's go get you checked out and cleaned up."

Then they could celebrate Christmas.

Together.

10:07 P.M.

"How are you doing?" Tom perched on the edge of the sofa where Hannah was sitting under a pile of blankets. She had been sitting there most of the day.

After he shot Jeff Shields to stop him from shooting Hannah, Chloe and the cops who had just arrived had come bursting in. They had confirmed that Jeff was dead. Paramedics had also turned up and Hannah had allowed herself to be checked out without much protest. After ERT had taken some photos of the blood and brain matter that was splattered all over her, the paramedics had taped a white square bandage over the small wound on her temple from where Jeff had dug the gun into her flesh.

While ERT processed the scene, agents took his and Hannah's statements. The shooting would be deemed justified. Chloe and six other agents and officers had been just outside the door and had seen that Jeff was about to shoot Hannah. He hadn't had a choice. It was Jeff or Hannah, and there was no way he was letting Hannah die.

When they'd given their statements and ERT was finished with Hannah, he had taken her upstairs and put her in a steaming hot bath. She'd still been shaking, and he couldn't stand seeing blood on her for a single second longer. After she was cleaned up, she had settled herself on one of the sofas in the living room, and since she was still shivering, he had collected several of the blankets in the house and bundled her up in them.

Chloe had organized getting the floor in Hannah's hall cleaned, and now the house was back to normal and empty of all but the two of them, for the first time since they'd gotten up this morning.

"I'm all right." She smiled at him. Her face was still a little haunted, and her eyes still held a glint of shock, but he knew she would make it through this just like she had worked her way through everything else that had been thrown her way.

"I was so scared," he admitted, cupping her cheek in his hand, his thumb absently stroking along her cheekbone. "I thought he was going to kill you."

"I thought he was going to kill *you*." Hannah lifted her hand to cover his.

"When you jabbed his wound and then twisted out of his grip, I was simultaneously terrified and impressed."

"I knew I just had to get away from the gun and you would take care of him."

Her complete and utter faith in him warmed him. He was glad it had worked out because it could just have easily ended with his and Hannah's dead bodies left lying on the floor for his partner to discover rather than Jeff's.

But it *had* worked out.

And he had Hannah back in his life.

This time, he wasn't going to let her go.

"I have something for you, an early Christmas gift," he told her.

Hannah's eyes brightened. "Yeah?"

He pulled a small black velvet box out of his pocket and dropped down onto one knee, reaching inside the blankets swaddling Hannah to pull out her left hand. "Hannah, will you marry me?"

Her eyes were as wide as saucers now. "Marry you? Now? We only just reconnected, maybe we should wait and see how things go."

"Do you love me?"

"Yes, of course. Always."

"I love you, too. I always have and I always will. We're stronger together, and we love each other. Why should we wait?"

"Okay." Hannah's face broke into a giant smile.

"Okay?" he repeated cautiously.

"Yes, I want to marry you again. I missed you so much."

Grinning, Tom leaned forward and kissed her, then took the ring from the box and slid it on to her finger.

"Oh, Tom." Hannah's eyes grew watery when she saw the ring. "You kept it."

"I did." When he and Hannah had divorced, she had given him back the engagement ring. He had kept it in a drawer in his bedroom, unable to part with it. It was as if his heart knew something his brain didn't. That one day he and Hannah would be thrown back together and given a second chance. A chance to fix what they'd let break and wind up together again.

"It's perfect," she gushed.

"I always loved you, Hannah. Always. I never wanted us to break up. I walked away because I thought it was what you wanted, that it was what you needed, that it was what was best for you. It tore me up inside, but I will always put your needs before my own."

"I've always loved you, too, Tom. I let you walk away because I thought it was what was best for you. I thought it was what you needed to heal from what happened. I hated letting you go. I wanted you to stay. I wanted you. But I couldn't let you be hurt by staying with me."

Tom curled his hands around the back of her neck and rested his forehead against hers. If only they had talked. "In the future, we communicate so we don't have another disastrous misunderstanding like that."

"We both shut each other out, and we won't do that again. We took a bad situation and made it so much worse because we were both too stubborn to sit down and talk to each other. But now we know better. We won't make that mistake again."

Keeping hold of her, he lifted his head so he could look her in the eye. "Let's get married tomorrow."

"Tomorrow? Tomorrow is Christmas Day."

"What better day to get married? You love Christmas, and it's a day of hope—of peace, reconciliation, and love. And I don't want to wait to make you my wife again. We lost three years. I don't want to lose another second."

"What would I wear? And who would marry us at such short notice? And what are we going to do about a reception?"

"You can wear the same dress you wore for our first wedding. You still have it, right?"

"I do."

"We don't need to worry about a wedding reception. We're going to be celebrating Christmas with our families tomorrow, anyway. It can be a Christmas and wedding celebration."

"Our families are going to think we're crazy," Hannah said. He could see in her face he almost had her convinced.

"We were going to go to church in the morning, anyway. I spoke with the minister at my parents' church. He said he'll perform the ceremony. We can do this, baby. We can get married tomorrow. We can rebuild the marriage that we had before. After the attack, we gave up on each other. We were both broken and we had a lot to work through, but we're stronger now, and we're ready to work on things, to make our marriage stronger than it ever was before. We're not going to let those men win. We're not going to let them destroy our love. I have something else for you."

"Another gift?"

"Yep." Tom pulled out an envelope from his pocket and handed it to Hannah.

She opened the envelope and took out what was inside. When she saw what it was, she grew teary again, "Oh, Tom. Does this mean what I think it means?"

"It does."

"It's perfect. The best gift you could have ever given me."

"You were right. I was a victim, too. And it's time to admit it and do something about it. That's the name of one of the trauma counselors the FBI refers victims to. I know you were going to look for a new therapist after learning what you did about Bryce McCracken, so I thought we could both go. Together and separately."

"I love you so much." She pulled his face closer so she could whisper her lips across his. "I was going to give this to you tomorrow, but I want you to have it now." Hannah unwrapped the blankets from around herself and went to the Christmas tree, retrieving a gift that was sitting underneath. Tom sat on the couch and Hannah returned and settled herself in his lap, handing him a green and red striped box, tied with glittery gold ribbon with a large bow on top. "I was going to give this to you the next Christmas we would have celebrated together. I kept it. For some reason, I couldn't get rid of it. It was like I somehow knew that we would find our way back to each other."

Intrigued, he opened the box, and his heart melted when he saw what was inside. "It's beautiful, Hannah." Carefully, he lifted the snow globe out. She'd gotten it specially made for him. Inside the glass dome was them. Him and Hannah. They were building a snowman, and the little model Tom had his arm around little model Hannah. They were in the yard of a house that looked just like the one they had always talked about buying. The little house had been decorated for Christmas with little lights around its eaves and a wreath on the door.

"Do you like it?" she asked.

"Sweetheart, I love it. Every time I look at it, I'm going to think of you." He pressed a kiss to her cheek. He had never loved a gift as much in his life as the one he held in his hands.

"Shake it." She beamed at him.

He did and snow filled the little world as it began to play a song, "Joy to the World." It was his favorite Christmas carol, because it reminded him of Hannah and her childish joy at Christmas time. He hugged her tightly. "You are the most amazing, beautiful, sweet, caring, kind, loving person on the planet."

Hannah giggled. "You just think that because you love me."

"I think it because it's true," he corrected. He kissed her, long and slow, relishing the feeling of the woman he loved in his arms, her arms around his neck, her lips on his. This was what life was all about, and right about now, he didn't think it could get any better than this.

When he finished kissing her, Hannah yawned. She'd held up amazingly well throughout the day, but now she needed rest.

"Bedtime." He scooped her up and deposited her on her feet.

"Wait, we can't, we have to get the milk and cookies first," she protested.

Tom chuckled. "You are too cute."

"Cute?" She made a face at him. "Thirty-year-old people are *not* cute."

"If you say so, babe." He grinned.

She rolled her eyes at him and hurried off to the kitchen, returning a moment later with a glass of milk, a chocolate chip cookie on a Santa plate, and a couple of carrots. "Here we go, snacks for Santa and his reindeer," she announced, setting them on a small table next to the Christmas tree.

He just laughed. He loved that Hannah still wanted to leave milk and cookies for Santa, even though she was an adult now and knew he didn't exist. He loved that spark of childish joy that still lived inside her, and he was so grateful that what she'd been through hadn't extinguished it.

"Go to bed." He swatted at her behind. "I'll be right up."

"Okay, don't be long. I'll be waiting."

The look she shot him before she sauntered out of the room was enough to have him quickly gobbling up the cookie, chewing on the carrots, and gulping down the milk so he could join his fiancée in bed. Making love to the woman who owned his heart, falling asleep with her in his arms, then waking up to tomorrow morning and making her his wife.

This was the best Christmas ever.

Epilogue

ONE YEAR LATER

December 25th
5:58 A.M.

"Wake up. Tom, wake up." Hannah shook her husband, trying to rouse him. Some nights he slept like a rock.

It was Christmas morning. She wanted to run downstairs, sit on the floor in front of their tree, and exchange gifts. Why was Tom always so hard to wake up when she wanted him awake, but whenever she wanted him to stay asleep, the tiniest noise woke him?

"Tom," she groaned.

"What?" came the groggy reply as he rolled over in bed.

"It's Christmas morning," she reminded him.

"And?" He looked like he was about ready to go straight back to sleep. He hadn't even opened his eyes yet.

"And I want you to get up." She poked him, and then when that didn't work, she straddled him and planted her lips against his, kissing him passionately. That had the desired effect. Tom blinked his eyes open, his hands came out from under the covers to grasp her hips, then tried to find their way inside her pajama pants. "Hey, none of that." She swatted them away.

"*You* kissed *me*," he pouted.

"Only to wake you up." She grinned, climbed off him, and grabbed his hand, pulling him out of the bed after her.

"Why are you so excited this morning?"

"Because it's Christmas."

Hannah practically ran down the stairs to the living room, where she went immediately to the small table beside the tree where she'd left milk and cookies for Santa and carrots for his reindeer. She was thirty-one now, much too old to leave snacks for Santa Claus on Christmas Eve, but she couldn't let go of the tradition from her childhood. She loved that Tom went along with it, playing the role of Santa and eating the snacks, just like her dad used to when she was a little girl.

"He came." She clapped her hands and held up the empty plate and glass for Tom to see.

He was standing watching her, looking almost impossibly hot as the sweat pants he slept in hung low on his hips, and his bare chest showed off his perfect abs. His eyes were twinkling merrily with amusement. "You're so cute when you do the Santa thing."

She poked her tongue out at him. "I am *not* cute."

"Oh, you are." He came to her, wrapped an arm around her waist and drew her against him. "Happy Anniversary, Mrs. Drake."

"Happy Anniversary, Mr. Drake." She kissed him, ending it when his wandering hands started to roam again. "Gift time." She extricated herself from his grip and sat down in front of the tree, reaching underneath for one particular gift.

"Why are you so peppy this morning?" he asked again as he joined her.

"I'm always peppy on Christmas morning."

"No, you're extra peppy today." He was looking at her suspiciously.

"You're just being paranoid." She ruffled his brown locks. "Here's your gift."

Looking no less suspicious, he took the box and opened it. "New Christmas stockings," he said as he pulled out the first one.

"So we can hang them on the mantle," she beamed. "See, yours has Santa Claus on it."

"And yours has Mrs. Claus," he said as he reached into the box and pulled it out. Then his eyes grew round. "Hannah."

Tears of joy filled her eyes, and she nodded. "Look in the box."

He lifted out the third Christmas stocking, and picked up the pregnancy test with blue and pink ribbon tied in a bow around it that was lying underneath. "You're pregnant," he put his hand on her stomach.

"Santa Claus, Mrs. Claus, and this time next year, we'll have a little baby Claus," she put her hand over his.

"I love you so much." He swept the back of his hand across her cheek then kissed her, tears in his eyes. Her big, strong, macho husband was crying.

"You're happy, right?" she asked, suddenly anxious. They hadn't talked about starting a family yet. They both knew they wanted one, but they hadn't discussed the timing.

"Ecstatic," he assured her. "This is the best gift you could ever have given me."

"This is the best Christmas ever." She smiled contently.

"You said that last Christmas," Tom reminded her.

"I was wrong."

"You betcha you were." Tom pulled her into his lap and kissed her again.

Hannah laid her head on his shoulder and snuggled closer. Four years ago, she had hit rock bottom, and she couldn't foresee a future where she was this happy. One year ago, she had been given a second chance, a chance to reclaim what she'd lost, to get her husband back. This year, she and Tom were celebrating their second first year anniversary with their baby growing inside her.

This really was the best Christmas ever.

Can Chloe and Fin overcome loss, grief, and anger to find their

way back to one another? Find out in the next book in this thrilling romantic suspense series!

Christmas Captive (Christmas Romantic Suspense #2)

Also by Jane Blythe

Detective Parker Bell Series

A SECRET TO THE GRAVE

WINTER WONDERLAND

DEAD OR ALIVE

LITTLE GIRL LOST

FORGOTTEN

Count to Ten Series

ONE

TWO

THREE

FOUR

FIVE

SIX

BURNING SECRETS

SEVEN

EIGHT

NINE

TEN

Broken Gems Series

CRACKED SAPPHIRE

Saving SEALs Series

SAVING RYDER

SAVING ERIC

SAVING OWEN

SAVING LOGAN

SAVING GRAYSON

SAVING CHARLIE

Prey Security Series

PROTECTING EAGLE

PROTECTING RAVEN

PROTECTING FALCON

PROTECTING SPARROW

PROTECTING HAWK

PROTECTING DOVE

Prey Security: Alpha Team Series

DEADLY RISK

LETHAL RISK

EXTREME RISK

FATAL RISK

COVERT RISK

SAVAGE RISK

Prey Security: Artemis Team Series

IVORY'S FIGHT

PEARL'S FIGHT

LACEY'S FIGHT

OPAL'S FIGHT

Prey Security: Bravo Team Series

VICIOUS SCARS

RUTHLESS SCARS

Christmas Romantic Suspense Series

CHRISTMAS HOSTAGE

CHRISTMAS CAPTIVE

CHRISTMAS VICTIM

YULETIDE PROTECTOR

YULETIDE GUARD

YULETIDE HERO

HOLIDAY GRIEF

Conquering Fear Series (Co-written with Amanda Siegrist)

DROWNING IN YOU

OUT OF THE DARKNESS

CLOSING IN

About the Author

USA Today bestselling author Jane Blythe writes action-packed romantic suspense and military romance featuring protective heroes and heroines who are survivors. One of Jane's most popular series includes Prey Security, part of Susan Stoker's OPERATION ALPHA world! Writing in that world alongside authors such as Janie Crouch and Riley Edwards has been a blast, and she looks forward to bringing more books to this genre, both within and outside of Stoker's world. When Jane isn't binge-reading she's counting down to Christmas and adding to her 200+ teddy bear collection!

To connect and keep up to date please visit any of the following

Printed in Great Britain
by Amazon

53337324R00115